GRANDPA FRANK'S GREAT BIG BUCKET LIST

JENNY PEARSON

Illustrated by David O'Connell

USBORNE

My name is Frank Davenport, just like my dad. And just like my grandpa. And this is the story of our Bucket List.

I f Dad had known what would happen by giving me his name, he wouldn't have called me Frank. He would have let my mum have her way and I'd be called something like Tarquin or Marmaduke or Montgomery and then I'd have a name that didn't fit my face. But Mum would have liked that, because she'd be able to introduce me to her new friends at her new tennis club and say, in her new "la-di-da" voice, "Everybody, this is my son, Tarquin." And I'd straighten my blazer and say, "Pleasure's all mine," or something like that.

Luckily for me, Dad got his way and I was named **Frank**. After **him** and **his dad** and **his dad's dad**.

5

And probably **his dad's dad's dad** too.

I think Dad used to like our family tradition, but when the step-grandmother he'd forgotten to tell me about (because of the Davenport family rift) died, she left behind all her money to Frank John Davenport.

And unluckily for Dad, that isn't his name. His name is Frank *James* Davenport.

I am Frank *John* Davenport.

And because of that, I ended up with £462,000 in a bank account and strict instructions to take care of Grandpa Frank Senior Senior – or **Grandpa Frank**, as I call him (because no one's got time to say "Senior Senior").

Of course, Mum and Dad were really keen to get the cash off me. When they weren't arguing with each other, they were trying to find some loophole in the law, so I'd have to give them the money. They didn't stop going on about it being a huge mistake. But as I see it, there must have been a good reason Grandma Nora left the cash to me and asked *me* to be the one to look after Grandpa Frank. And I'm not the kind of kid who ignores the last request of a dead step-grandmother, even if I never met her. I'm the kind of kid who takes that kind of instruction seriously. Very seriously.

So this is the story of what I did with all that money. This is the story of our **Bucket List** and the things I've learned along the way. Like old people are actually quite buoyant when dunked in water and true happiness doesn't come with a price tag.

CHAPTER 1

Monkeys are hard to come by

The day I found out about the money from Grandma Nora, Dad had somehow come into a little bit of his own. And, what with it being Friday and the last day before the summer holidays, he picked me up early from school.

There was a class party, but I didn't mind missing it. It was probably going to be a bit lame anyway. I didn't get my yearbook signed but I wasn't too worried about that. I'd only been at St Margaret's a couple of terms, following our most recent move, and the mates I had managed to make weren't really talking to me at that precise moment in time. My dad had sold their dads a load of knock-off aftershave which had dyed their faces purple. The purple faces were one thing, but it turned out most of the boys in my year had sploshed it under their armpits and Tyler Scott had basically bathed in the stuff. He turned up to school looking like an angry Ribena berry, and Tyler Scott is the kind of kid who has the final say regarding who's in and who's out. And I was out.

When Dad turned up at school, I was practising keepy-uppies while the rest of my year were playing a game of football on the yard. Dad said he was keen to spend an afternoon with me, and as that didn't happen often, I was feeling pretty chuffed. I wasn't *too* bothered about sticking around.

"Too smashing a day to be cooped up in there, Frank. The sun is shining, the birds are tweeting. It's a day for a father to spend time with his favourite son," he said, ruffling my hair with his fingers.

"Ah, gerroff." I knocked his hand away even though I didn't really mind him doing it. "Favourite son? I'm your only son."

"Well, you should be glad you're not my second favourite then." He laughed and plonked his arm on my head like I was some sort of resting post. "Let's bust you out of here; I've signed you out with the bloke on reception."

"Oi!" I said, ducking out the way as we buzzed ourselves out of the school gate. "Where are we going?"

I was really hoping for a kickabout in the park, but he said, "Going to teach you a little something you won't be learning in school. A little something about '**The Sell**'." He pulled a wodge of tenners out of his back pocket, held them up to my face and said, "Sniff it. Get a good lungful. Now, tell me, what's that smell of?"

I breathed in, but before I could answer he smacked me round the chops with the bundle of notes and said,

"What you're smelling there – and there's no better smell – is the **smell of success**."

I wasn't too sure about that. Smelled a bit funny to me, like the school stock cupboard. But the smell wasn't really what I was thinking about. I was thinking about *how* my dad had suddenly got to be so flush. Mum was not going to be happy if he was up to his old tricks. She'd been on at him for ages about getting a proper job.

"Where did you get all that from?" I said, trying to keep up with his pace.

"Ask me no questions, son, and I'll tell you no lies." He gave me a wink and a big smile when he said that. I grinned back. I couldn't help myself. It's just the way my dad is, see. A proper charmer, Mum used to say. There was a time when that wink and smile used to work on her too. Not so much these days though.

Dad folded the notes back into his wallet and stuck it in his coat pocket. "There's nothing more important in this world than money, Frank, and don't you forget it."

"What are you going to do with it?"

"I'm going to invest it."

"Invest it?" Experience told me that we were not heading off to the bank.

"There's a job lot of spangly pony toys going for a quid each. I'll mark them up to a fiver, sell them at the school gates this afternoon. You know, get in on the end-of-term excitement? Just you wait, I'll change this hundred into a monkey—"

"A monkey? I've always wanted a monkey!" I like all animals actually, but monkeys are a particular favourite.

Dad slapped me on the back and laughed. "Nah, Frank, you wally. A monkey is five hundred quid. Not an *actual* monkey. Who'd want an actual monkey?"

Daft question, but I answered anyway. "Er, I think you mean who *wouldn't* want an actual monkey."

Dad said, "Not easy to get your hands on primates, son." Like he'd had a go at it before. Then he said, "You watch and learn, son. I'm going to sell those 'petite ponies' outside St Margaret's, make a packet, and then what I'm going to do is buy your mother something she'd really like. Get back in her good books."

As it happened, the little spangly ponies weren't the genuine article. They looked more like little over-worked donkeys, but Dad was right – it was all about **"The Sell"**.

And, boy, can my dad *sell*.

"Basically, son," he said, putting his arm around me, "you need to make people believe they want what you've got. Make them think you're offering them something they can't get elsewhere. That it's a once in a lifetime opportunity that they'd be daft to miss out on."

I wasn't sure how colourful toy ponies were a once in a lifetime opportunity, but it turned out Dad was right when he said, "Your words are more powerful than the product, Frank."

He made those donkeys seem like glittering stallions and he shifted the lot. He was in a top mood after that. I'd probably still have preferred a game of footie in the park to practise my step-overs, but he was all smiles and swagger when we walked into Argos later that day. He told the man that he wanted the best washer-dryer money could buy and even paid extra to get it delivered immediately.

On the way home, he bought me a bottle of pop from the newsagent's – the kind Mum never lets me have because she says there's no such thing as a blue raspberry. Dad took a swig of his Irn-Bru and said, "Us Davenports are born winners, Frank. You hear what I'm saying?"

I heard what he was saying, but I'd seen enough purple armpits to have my doubts.

And I was right to be doubtful, because when we got home Mum was standing on the doorstep wearing her leopard-print silk dressing gown over her Grigsby's supermarket uniform, looking beautiful and angry all at once. It didn't take a genius to work out what was wrong with her, because she was holding a small yellow horse in her hand.

Before Dad could speak, Mum held the toy up, lifted its tail and a truly terrifying dinosaur-type roar seemed to come out of its mouth. "The phone has been ringing off the hook, Frank. Susanna Montgomery doubts her little Fiona will get a wink of sleep tonight because she's so traumatized by this horrifying horse toy you sold her at the school gates."

I couldn't suppress a snigger, but Dad's usually confident smile wavered ever so slightly before he said, "Added bonus, that – audio!"

Mum shot him – and for some reason *me* – a withering look. "What am I going to do with you two?"

"Make us a cuppa?" Dad suggested, which, from the look on Mum's face, didn't seem to go down that well.

Her mouth was opening really wide like she was about to shout, but at that moment the delivery van turned up, and her red lips snapped shut. She raised her left eyebrow – the angry one – and said suspiciously, "What's that?"

Dad's chest puffed up. "It's a gift for you, Tanya – a brand-new washer-dryer. Thought you deserved it."

I thought that might win her over, but for some reason she didn't seem that delighted.

Her eyes narrowed. "You thought I deserved a washer-dryer? That some kind of joke, Frank?" She hollered over to the men who were lowering it off the back of the delivery lorry. "You can take that back to whatever dodgy place it's come from."

Dad said, "It's come from Argos. It says it right there in two-metre lettering on the side of the truck."

Which seemed like a reasonable enough answer, but she stepped back into the house and slammed the door.

Dad looked at me with his twinkly eyes and said, "You know what your mother sounds like?" Then he lifted the tail of his **My Little Dinosaur Donkey** and it did its fearsome roar.

We were both still laughing when Mum opened the door and said, "I heard that," which shut us up pretty smartish.

Then she said, "You, inside."

Dad took a step forward, but Mum held up her hand. "Not you – *him*." Which I took to mean me because I was the only other person there, so I stepped past her.

"You, darling," she said to Dad, "need to go and sort out your latest mess or I really will roar at you."

Dad was still in the middle of saying, "Consider it sorted, light of my life," when she slammed the door again.

Mum did this massive sigh and rolled her eyes. "Honestly! That man!"

My dad isn't perfect, and Mum has her faults too. I suppose we all do. But even though they argue – *a lot* – they love each other. Dad didn't need to give Mum household appliances to prove it. It was a shame he didn't seem to realize that though – it could have saved us all a lot of trouble in the long run.

CHAPTER 2

It's okay to lie to strange blokes in shiny suits

After Dad had disappeared, Mum received another angry phone call from a dino-donkey customer, which only added to her bad mood. She stormed into the kitchen and opened the fridge door like she was trying to rip it off its hinges. Then she slammed the carton of tropical **Fruity Juicy** onto the worktop like she was trying to smash it into smithereens and said, "You want some?" like, if I didn't, she might try and force it down my throat anyway.

I said, "Yeah," because I thought that was the safest answer in the circumstances.

"'Yeah' what, young man? One afternoon with your

dad and all your manners disappear?" She waved the juice carton and a load of orange liquid sloshed over the floor tiles. "Now look what he's made me do! His schemes will be the end of me! Why he can't get a regular job I'll never know! And imagine selling them at the school gates to your new friends – what was he thinking?"

She slammed the carton back onto the worktop and more juice slopped out. "So what do you say?"

I gulped. "Yes please, wonderful mother. I would like some **Fruity Juicy** juice. If there is any left, that is."

She poured me a glassful and sighed. "Sorry, you know how he winds me up. This toy thing! And buying a washer-dryer! I *have* a washer-dryer – it might be old and need a bit of a kick to get it started, but it does the job. What I need is the debts—" She stopped. "You don't need to hear this." She grabbed my face and pulled it towards her and said, "Tell me, my handsome boy, how was your Year Six party?"

I did not mind her calling me handsome, but I did have an issue with her total disregard for personal space. So I wiggled out of her grasp. "Dunno."

"What do you mean, you don't know?"

"Didn't go to it. Dad picked me up early."

"He did what?!" She shouted this so loudly that I jumped, and a bit of tropical jungle juice shot out of my nose, which wasn't ideal.

"Tell me you got your yearbook signed at least. I was on the organizing committee for that. And it wasn't easy, with all those judgy women judging me because their husbands had to go to their nice jobs looking like purple Smurfs since your father sold them that aftershave."

I couldn't help but chuckle at that image and I noticed Mum was trying not to smile too. She rolled her eyes and said, "It's not funny, Frank," even though it was. "Now, tell me about your yearbook – what happened?"

I shrugged. "It doesn't matter. I'm not bothered." I didn't want to admit that nobody would have wanted to sign it anyway. "Dad taught me all about '**The Sell**' instead."

Mum closed her eyes and said quietly, "Give me strength."

I don't know who she was talking to, but I hoped whoever it was didn't give her any. She's strong enough as it is.

When she opened her eyes again, she said, "It *does* matter, Frank," and then she stroked my cheek. She sounded a bit upset, which made me wonder if she was right about it mattering, but I didn't want to think too much about that.

"And **The Sell**? I can't believe what I'm hearing." She pointed her finger at me in quite a threatening manner. "*You* are going to get a proper job when you're older."

I said, "Like being a footballer for Charlton Athletic or a zookeeper?" But I don't think she heard me because she carried on ranting.

"I can't believe he took you out of school to flog demon donkeys. And back at school of all places. Do you know what I'd like to do to him right now?"

The doorbell rang and I thought I might be spared knowing what Mum would like to do to Dad, but she said, "If it's him with that washer-dryer, I swear I'll stick him in it and wash him on an extra-hot high-speed cycle and boil the stupid out of him."

Luckily for us all, it wasn't Dad at the front door. It was some bloke wearing a shiny navy suit that you could tell had set him back a few quid.

"Is this the residence of a Mr Frank Davenport?"

I could tell right away he was proper posh. Not posh like Mum pretended to be when she was at school meetings or down at the tennis club she'd recently joined.

Mum leaned against the door frame, patted her puffy blonde hair behind her ears and put on her hoity-toity accent. "And who is enquiring?"

We'd both got used to screening any unexpected visitors for Dad so we didn't have to face any unwanted callers who wanted a *chat* about something he'd been up to.

"I've come from J L Winterson solicitors."

Mum began to close the door and, sounding like Mum again, said, "Look, we're separated," which was a lie, but I still didn't like hearing it. "If he's sold you something you want to return, there's no point coming to me. Haven't seen him for months."

Milliseconds before the latch clicked, sharp-suit managed to blurt out, "Mrs Davenport, I'm afraid you are mistaken, I am here to—"

Mum does not like being told she's mistaken about anything, so she swung the door open again with more force than was strictly necessary. The poor bloke almost leaped out of his designer shoes.

"Are you telling me you know better than I do when I last saw my husband?"

"I...I..."

"I wouldn't even know how to get hold of him if you asked me." She turned to me for backup. "Isn't that right, Frank?"

"That's right, Mum." I'm not a big one for lying but I know the drill. Davenports look out for each other. And besides, it doesn't count if you're lying to posh blokes in flash suits.

The guy cowered a little, which is understandable because Mum can be a bit scary when she's worked up. She's only small but, as Dad says, she's also magnificent.

He pulled at the knot of his polka-dot tie and said, "Mrs Davenport, forgive me for any offence I may inadvertently have caused." He said it all polite like that. "But I have not come to demand money, more to give it."

That caught Mum out. It caught me out too. It's not every day some guy with really shiny shoes and weirdly bouncy hair shows up, wanting to give you money.

"I think, if you were to be so kind as to let me in, you would find what I have got to say very agreeable – very agreeable indeed."

I was all for it, but Mum needed more convincing. "What do you mean, 'agreeable'? No one hands over money for nothing. What's the catch?"

"I'm not sure it would be delicate to discuss such matters on the doorstep."

Mum raised her angry left eyebrow to let him know that was exactly what they'd be doing.

"Very well, if you insist." He cleared his throat. "I have come to discuss a substantial amount of money that has been left in a last will and testament."

That got her attention. I must have looked confused, because she said, "It's instructions about who someone is going to leave their money to after they've died."

And that got my attention too.

I started thinking about all the things I could buy with a substantial amount of money. For some reason, a monkey was the first thing that popped into my head.

Mum's angry eyebrow lowered slightly. "How substantial are we talking?"

Looking back now, I'm not proud that neither Mum nor I had bothered to ask who had died yet.

Anyway, the answer to the question we *had* bothered to ask – the *how substantial* question – was, "Considerably."

That made Mum open the door. "I think you had better come in, Mr... Sorry, I didn't catch your name."

"Mr Foster."

"Mr Foster, please do come in."

Her fancy voice was back out again.

"I should say, Mrs Davenport, we will need your husband to be present for this."

Mum looked at me through heavy eyelids and, apparently forgetting she was being posh again, said in a tired-sounding voice, "Frank, get your dad on the phone, will you?"

Mr Foster's forehead crunkled like a line of lying-down question marks. "But I thought you didn't know how to contact him?"

Mum smiled her big lipstick smile – the one that makes most people give her what she wants – and said, "Oh, Mr Foster, I don't remember saying that. I think you must be mistaken. Now come and sit down. Tea? Coffee?"

I called Dad and told him about the solicitor and the will and the considerably substantial amount of money and he turned up twenty minutes later with a Tesco bag full of brightly coloured, roaring miniature ponies and a hungry look in his eyes. We all gathered in the living room and Mum put a tray full of Mr Kipling cakes on the glass coffee table, which I was delighted about because we never have cake and I hadn't been allowed to eat in the living room since Mum had bought her fluffy white rug. I'd shovelled down two French Fancies and a Cherry Bakewell before Mr Foster had even opened his briefcase. The way I see it is that you've got to take your opportunities when they arrive. Anyway, I was very excited about what was happening and at that point I still didn't even know *exactly* how brilliantly things were going to turn out for me.

Mr Foster pulled out a thick yellowing envelope and said, "This is the last will and testament of Nora Louise Davenport."

I pulled a face. "Who?"

And Dad said, very matter-of-factly, "My stepmother. Your step-grandmother, I suppose."

"I have a step-grandmother?"

"Well, not any more, you don't."

"But I *had* a step-grandmother. You didn't think that this was information worth sharing with me?"

Dad shrugged like it was no biggie, and said, "You never asked." Like asking about dead step-grandparents was a regular topic of conversation.

"But, Dad—"

"Frank, son, shall we talk about this later? It's family business. Let's hear what Mr Foster here has to say about this considerably substantial sum of money."

Mr Foster glanced at his expensive-looking watch and said, "Yes, I am keen to commence proceedings."

Dad got himself comfortable in his armchair and

squeezed Mum's hand and said, "Love, this might be the answer to all our troubles. Maybe the old boot has finally done something good by me."

I thought the "old boot" comment was a bit strong in the circumstances, but Mum didn't seem to notice. She tried to be all sensible and said, "Shhh, let's hear what Mr Foster has to say," but I could tell she was just as excited as Dad.

Mr Foster did a little cough and began. He looked at Dad and said, in a very serious voice, "I, Nora Louise

Davenport…" which made me snigger because he didn't look much like a Nora.

He gave me a sharp look and continued. "…bequeath the sum of **£462,000** to Frank John Davenport."

And that's when I almost choked on my Lemon Layered Slice.

Because *I* was Frank *John* Davenport.

I could buy a monkey after all.

I could buy a whole wagon-load of monkeys if I wanted.

CHAPTER 3

If you want to ignore an argument, eat a French Fancy

No one said anything for a while as we all tried to make sense of my sudden and unexpected fortune. For some reason, my new-found riches did not appear to be magical news to my parents' ears.

Eventually, Mum stood up and started pacing around on the fluffy white rug that we weren't supposed to wear our shoes on, saying over and over, "There has to be a mistake. You can't leave that sort of money to an eleven-year-old child."

Dad kicked the bag of little ponies across the room. It hit the wall and they all started roaring. Then he covered his face with his hands and said, "This is typical. Just typical. She's probably gone and done that on purpose to spite me."

I, however, was having a much nicer time. I was stuffing my face with cake and grinning and thinking, *Four hundred and sixty-two thousand smackeroonies! AWESOME!* I wasn't sure because I'm not that good at rounding big numbers, but I thought it might be pretty near **half a million quid**. I could definitely get a season ticket for Charlton with that sort of cash.

From all the differing reactions in the room, Mr Foster worked out that there must have been some kind of mistake. He pointed at me and said, "*You're* Frank John Davenport? I assumed that would be your father."

"Nope. Dad's Frank *James* Davenport." It really was pretty hard not to sound too pleased about how things had turned out.

Mr Foster seemed a bit flustered when I said that. "Ah, goodness. Well, if I remember correctly, there is something left for a Frank James Davenport too."

Mum stopped trampling and Dad dropped his hands away from his face.

"Go on," they said at the same time.

Mr Foster studied the important-looking paperwork. "Now let me see...hmm." He flipped it over. "It's here somewhere. Ah, yes. Here we go."

Mum and Dad's eyes had never looked so big and goggly!

"To Frank James Davenport I leave my collection of jigsaws, Humpledink the teddy and the sum of £230 to be delivered on or after your eighteenth birthday."

Dad put his face back in his hands and Mum steadied herself against the mantelpiece.

Mr Foster looked up at Dad and gave a weak smile. "Well, you won't have to wait for the £230, as you appear to be well past eighteen."

It must have completely sucked to be Dad right then.

But it was pretty awesome to be me. I was suddenly the richest kid I knew. Well, money-wise anyway.

"Look," Dad said, and he grabbed Mr Foster by the jacket sleeve. "This is obviously a mistake. The **£462,000** was meant for me, any fool can see that."

Mr Foster yanked his arm free. "We have to work to the law, Mr Davenport. And the law is on Frank John Davenport's side."

I was pleased that Mr Foster said the law was on my side. I had a feeling Dad would never get the law on his side. Not with his history of selling questionable goods. Which meant the money was as good as mine.

Mum said, in a voice that was caught somewhere between a laugh and a scream, "You can't give a child **£462,000**. He'll just spend it on comics and computer games."

I thought, *I won't, I'm going to spend it on footie gear and monkeys*, but I didn't say that. I just felt a bit angry that she was trying to ruin it for me.

"Actually," Mr Foster said, "the money does come with an instruction on what it should be used for."

My heart sank a little bit, because something told me that wasn't going to be a pair of top-of-the-range footie boots *or* a basketful of monkeys.

Mr Foster held up the letter again. "The sum of **£462,000** should primarily be used to ensure the continuing care and well-being of Frank Ernest Davenport, who resides at Autumnal Leaves Residential Home."

"Who?" I asked for the second time that day.

"That", Dad said with a sigh, "is your grandpa."

"I have a grandpa too?" This was unbelievable.

"You know you have a grandpa," Dad said, like that would make it true. "It's just him and I don't speak, that's all."

Maybe I'd forgotten, but I was pretty sure that Dad hadn't spoken about him before. I know now that was because he didn't like talking about what had happened between them.

"I didn't know! I swear! Are there any other relations you've forgotten to tell me about? I haven't got a second cousin hidden under the stairs or an uncle stashed in the shed, have I?"

Dad rolled his eyes. "Don't be daft, Frank."

"Uncle Vinny would never fit in the shed, not with all those bagless bagpipes your father still hasn't managed to sell," Mum said quite pointedly.

"Just waiting for the right buyer, love," Dad said quite unconvincingly. "Look, Frank, I must have mentioned your grandfather."

"Yeah, maybe, but you always made it sound like he was dead."

"Son, you have a **Grandpa Frank** who is still alive. Happy?"

I thought about it and realized I was. I had gained **£462,000 and a new grandpa** in the space of an afternoon. Unfortunately, I had also gained a dead step-grandma, but I guess you can't win them all.

Mr Foster did a little cough. "There is more, if I could continue."

Dad threw his hands in the air. "Do carry on. I can hardly contain my excitement. What else is there? She left me a BMX or a lifetime supply of strawberry shoelaces?"

I don't know why he said it like that would be a bad thing.

Mr Foster handed me an envelope. "No, along with the will, there's a letter for Mr Frank John Davenport. It may explain things more clearly."

Dad said, "Go on then, son. Read it out. What are you waiting for?"

I opened it up and read it out loud.

Dear Frank,
At the end of my life I find myself with only one regret. And that is the rift I caused in your family. Now, with Frank Senior on his own and not always in full possession of all his faculties, I leave you this money to look after him. He doesn't think he needs anybody. But like most things, he's wrong about that. Please show him the care he needs and, if you do, I promise there will be a reward for you too.
Yours, Nora Davenport

Nobody said anything for a bit. I guess there was a lot to take in.

Eventually Dad said, "I can't believe the nerve of that woman, talking about rifts from beyond the grave. As far as I'm concerned, she's the reason Dad walked out on us. Can't ever forgive him or her for that."

For some reason, I was getting the distinct impression that Dad wasn't a massive fan of Step-grandma Nora. Not like me. I thought she was fantastic and probably very wise in her choice of who to leave all her cash to.

Mum said, "What do you think the reward is? Money? It's got to be more money."

I hoped it was money. Things were looking pretty good for me at that moment in time. I'd gained **£462,000**, a new grandad – which was nice, as my other one lived in the Costa del Sol – and the chance of a further reward, and it wasn't even teatime.

Mr Foster stood up and brushed the crumbs off his trousers. "I'll leave you good people to digest this information and see if I can find out more about this mysterious reward. In the meantime, if you could provide me with bank account details for yourself, Mr Davenport, I shall see about the transfer of the £230."

I put my hand up and said, "Excuse me, what about my **£462,000**?"

"Mrs Davenport set up a bank account in the name of Frank John Davenport before she passed. A card should arrive in the post in a few days."

"What sort of card?"

"A debit card."

This was excellent news. I'd have a debit card that would give me access to a bank account containing **£462,000**. The last time I'd felt this lucky was when I found a quid in a locker at the swimming pool, bought a Twix from the vending machine and two fell out.

Mum still wasn't pleased for me though. She looked at Mr Foster in the exact same way she'd looked at her washer-dryer gift. "You cannot be serious! You can't give an eleven-year-old kid a debit card to a bank account containing **almost half a million quid.** And you can't expect him to look after an elderly man. Frank, say something!"

I said, "To be honest, I don't have a problem with it."

"Not you, Frank, you wally. Your dad. I knew this same-name thing was going to be a problem when your father suggested it! But in all my imaginings, I never thought it would be this bad."

Dad ignored the same-name comment and said, "Mr Foster, my wife is right. This is ridiculous."

Mr Foster must have sensed things were on the turn

because he took a large step backwards into the hallway. "That may be so, but that is a matter for you to bring up with the courts. I suggest if you wish to contest the will, you go through the proper legal channels."

"And how much is that gonna cost us?" Mum snapped.

But Mr Foster didn't answer because he had already scarpered out the front door.

I ate every last exceedingly good Kipling delight while Mum and Dad argued about what they were going to do to get my money from me and then claim the reward for themselves. As far as I was concerned, they could try what they liked. They weren't getting any of it. Mr Foster had said the law was on my side. So I blocked out the shouting and thought about what I was going to spend my cash on, other than football stuff and a pet monkey.

But then I remembered my dead step-grandmother's instruction to look after Grandpa Frank. I didn't need flash footie boots. Or a monkey to play with. I had a brand-new undead grandpa instead and I was going

to look after him so brilliantly that the surprise reward would be as good as mine too. All I had to do was track my Grandpa Frank down, which I was certain was going to be way easier than catching a monkey, on account of old people not moving so fast. And besides, I had a lead –

Autumnal Leaves Residential Home.

CHAPTER 4

Even if you don't wear clean underpants every day, tell your mum you do

While Mum and Dad plotted against me and yelled at each other about whose plot was best, I went up to my room to google the price of monkeys, just out of interest. But instead, I found myself on the Autumnal Leaves Residential Home website. It turned out it was only half an hour away from our house. I couldn't believe it. We'd moved to a place right near my grandpa and no one had thought to mention it. I suppose we'd moved in a bit of a rush. My parents hadn't told me exactly why, but from the conversations I'd overheard, Dad had borrowed some money from people and couldn't pay it back.

Anyway, I admit I was more than a bit annoyed by this new information regarding the close proximity of Grandpa Frank, so I stomped down the stairs to have it out with them. I stormed into the living room just as Mum was shouting where she'd really like to put her new washer-dryer, which I guessed wasn't in the utility room. Dad shouted back that he knew plenty of women who would love a new washer-dryer, which even I knew wasn't the best line of defence.

I didn't wait for a break in all the shouting, I just shouted too. "Autumnal Leaves Residential Home is less than half an hour from here."

I think they'd forgotten about me because they both looked dead shocked to see me standing there. Neither of them said anything so I tried again. "Half an hour. I've got grandparents half an hour from here. You should have said when we moved here!"

"Strictly speaking, son, you've got one grandparent half an hour from here."

Mum walloped Dad on the arm and scowled. "Be a little more sensitive." Then she said, "Frank, we didn't tell you because your dad and your grandpa don't really get on. They haven't spoken in years because of what happened."

I looked at Dad. "Why wouldn't you speak to your dad for years?"

"Because I won't ever forgive *that man* for walking out on his family. He left us and never came back."

"Does he know about me?" I asked. "Does he even know I exist?"

"I'm sure someone would have told him," Dad said.

I crossed my arms to show them I meant business. "I want to see my Grandpa Frank – especially now I'm in charge of him and all. I need to start looking after him brilliantly if I want that extra reward."

It might seem to you that all I was interested in was the cash, and I suppose that was probably at the front of my mind, but I was also keen to have a grandparent. Other kids had them, and I didn't see why I couldn't have one too.

Dad put his hand on my shoulder. "Look, son, I know you think you'll be coming into all that money, but despite what Mr Foster says, it belongs to me and your mother."

I took a step back. "No, it doesn't. It's mine. It belongs to me. The law says it does. And Grandpa Frank belongs to me too!"

Dad laughed, which annoyed me a bit, and said, "He certainly isn't a pet, son."

I hadn't been thinking about him as a pet. Not really.

Then Mum said, "You can't even be trusted to be in charge of putting on clean underpants every day. Why would you want to be in charge of an old man you don't even know? No, it's simply not happening."

I didn't say it was because I'd rather be anywhere than listening to them arguing. Or that I had nothing else to do that summer because I had no mates thanks to Dad and his ridiculous get-rich-quick schemes. And I didn't say I was done waiting by the tennis court while Mum perfected her backhand with her coach, super-tanned Tony. That I was done with them not paying me any attention. That I was done feeling so alone. I was always an afterthought to them. They were too busy worrying about themselves to worry about me.

But I didn't say any of that. I didn't even say anything about the reward. I just said, "That's outrageous!

I ALWAYS wear clean underpants, lady!" which wasn't a complete lie. Then I stomped back upstairs.

As far as I was concerned, Mum and Dad could say all they wanted, but my mind was set. I had an instruction to look after my grandfather and, in my opinion, if you're supposed to look after someone then you had better do it. It wasn't my problem that Mum and Dad didn't realize that.

When I slammed the door behind me, I immediately felt like smashing up my bedroom, but I decided that would just end in me breaking a load of my stuff and feeling a bit stupid. So instead of doing something destructive, I decided to do something productive.

I phoned Autumnal Leaves.

A nice-sounding man with a soft floaty voice answered the phone. "Hello, Stephen speaking, this is Autumnal Leaves Residential Home, I would be delighted if I could be of assistance to you today."

Delighted – that sounded promising.

"Hello, Stephen, my name is Frank Davenport and I was hoping that I could drop by and see my grandpa, also called Frank Davenport, who I didn't know about.

See, I have been instructed to look after him and I have a whole truckload of money to help me do it."

There was a loud gasp down the phone and a very not-soft-or-floaty voice said, "A grandson? I did not know there was a grandson! I'm sure Mr Davenport would just love to see you. Dear old Frank has not been himself since his wife passed a few months ago. Please do drop in when you can. Visiting hours are nine to five, Monday to Sunday. I'll let him know you're coming, shall I?"

"Maybe don't. Keep it as a surprise. I'll come tomorrow."

"A surprise grandson, with a truckload of money, visiting tomorrow! This is simply marvellous news! I'm sure Frank will be thrilled to meet you. It will make his weekend!"

I decided Stephen was right. It *was* marvellous news. Even though I didn't really admit it to myself at the time, I was made up that I wouldn't have to spend the summer on my own. I could turn up the next day and start looking after my grandpa straight away. I bet he would be thrilled, we'd do some excellent bonding and I'd get my hands on that reward in no time. Sure, I had as much idea about how to look after an old person as I did a monkey, but that only worried me for a nanosecond. Because *really*, how hard could it be?

CHAPTER 5

Two life skills you need to master are: 1. Whistling loudly 2. A pull-up

Believe me

The following morning was the official start of the summer holidays and I was feeling far more positive than I had ever thought possible. Before, I had resigned myself to kicking a ball about the park or playing computer games on my own, but now I was rich. **And. It. Felt. Awesome.**

Dad had left early to "see a man about a dog", which is what he says when he doesn't want anyone to know what he's up to. And as it was Mum's day off, it meant she was heading to the tennis club. She'd won a six-month pass in a competition she didn't remember entering. I hadn't thought tennis would be her thing, to be honest, but she had really got into it.

After she'd planted one of her big lipstick kisses on me and disappeared out of the door to go and learn how to volley from her tennis coach, Tony with the mega-tan, I caught the bus to Autumnal Leaves. My parents are pretty relaxed about me heading out by myself now I've left primary school. As long as I stay local and keep myself out of trouble.

I couldn't wait until I got my bank card because then I'd be able to pay for a taxi to take me. Or a helicopter even. Or maybe I could go by camel. I've always wanted a ride on a camel. I made a mental note to find out how much camel-rental would cost.

Once I'd arrived, I looked down the gravel path at the front entrance of Autumnal Leaves and said out loud, "I'm here, Grandpa Frank, and I'm going to look after you."

As I walked along the drive, I began to think that whoever had named the place had a bit of a relaxed relationship with the truth. Because if you'd asked me what I'd expect to find at a place called Autumnal Leaves, I'd say trees. But there wasn't a single tree. Not even a bush, in actual fact. Autumnal Leaves was just a big grey brick building. There's not much else I can say to describe it, other than it looked really depressing. It probably didn't help that I was a little bit nervous, but I pushed those feelings to one side, because I had an important job to do.

The pale-skinned man with very messy hair who was sat at the reception desk didn't look up when I walked in through the automatic doors. He had ink on the side of his mouth where he'd been chewing his biro and seemed to be concentrating very hard on something. He still didn't look up when I stood right in front of the desk. He just carried on staring at what I could see by then was a crossword and mumbled, "Two words, first word six letters, second word two letters, means *I beg your pardon*."

He had a name badge on that said *Stephen*, so I reckoned it was highly probable he was the same person I'd spoken to on the phone the night before. As he didn't look like he was going to figure out the clue any time soon, I said, dead polite and all, "Excuse me—"

And he said, "That's it! Excuse me!" and wrote it in the squares. Then he looked at me and said, "Well done, you clever boy!"

For a moment, I didn't know what to say – the *clever boy* comment had come as a bit of a surprise. I don't think I'd ever been called a clever boy before and, I admit, I kind of liked it. Eventually I remembered why I was there and said, "I'm Frank Davenport, I spoke to you yesterday about coming in to see my grandpa."

He put his crossword down and smiled, revealing a chipped front tooth. "So you're the grandson with the truckload of money." He rose to his feet and looked me up and down and I felt a bit like he was asking me to prove it.

"I don't have it here, if that's what you're thinking."

He laughed and his eyes went all crinkly in a friendly kind of way.

"Now, I can't tell you how pleased I am to see you! A visitor is exactly what the old boy needs. Since Mrs Davenport passed, he's been a right Norman-No-Laughs. You just head straight through those double doors, carry on through the games room. He's in the lounge, *not* painting. It's art this morning and the theme is '**paint what makes you happy**'."

I looked at the doors. It was weird to think that my grandpa was on the other side. I suddenly felt a little wobble of worry. What if I was rubbish at looking after him? What if he didn't like me? What if he wouldn't even see me because of the fallout he'd had with Dad?

Stephen must have sensed my hesitation, because he said, "Go on, lad. You've got nothing to worry about."

It turns out he was wrong about that...but his words spurred me on. I strode off down the corridor, through the games room, which was basically a room with two old men asleep around a chessboard, and I marched into the lounge with way more confidence than I should have had.

I'd heard that old people smell funny and I can confirm there was definitely a funky scent that hit me when I entered the room. I'm not saying it was a *bad* smell as such. Just a bit weird. If you were to pin me down to describe it, I'd say it was a bit like steamed broccoli and antiseptic wipes.

The lounge wasn't exactly what I'd call an uplifting environment. It had a faded red carpet, a load of settees and high-backed chairs and a ton of old people dotted around the place like geriatric confetti. Some were painting, some were sleeping, some were reading, some knitting. Some were just sitting there, staring at nothing, which was a bit freaky. It was dead quiet, except for a few coughs, the clacking of knitting needles and an occasional "Blast!" from one old woman who was struggling to paint what looked like a pterodactyl. Which was an odd choice, considering the theme of **paint what makes you happy.**

I scanned all the old folk, looking for **Frank Senior Senior**, and that's when it dawned on me – I hadn't a scooby what my grandpa looked like. He could have been literally any one of the wrinklies in there. I'll admit it, this was a bit of an oversight on my part.

For a moment I was stumped about what to do. I thought about going round them all and asking every single one of them if they were Frank Davenport. That seemed a bit like hard work, so instead I just said, quite loudly because they were probably all a bit deaf, "Excuse me, are any of you Frank Davenport?"

No response.

I tried again, but not one of them looked up. So I stuck my fingers in my mouth and whistled. I'm good at whistling – Dad taught me how. It's an important and necessary life skill, he reckons. Like being able to do a pull-up, in case you ever end up dangling off a cliff edge – or the roof of a multistorey car park by a bloke you'd double-crossed, in Dad's case.

I still didn't get much of a reaction, which was a surprise because I'm known for the impressive volume of my whistles. One old woman, who was sitting in a wheelchair with a blanket over her knees, looked up from her painting of what could have been a giant brown ant or a horse and said, "You say something, poppet?"

I said, "Yes, I asked if any of you lot were **Frank Davenport Senior Senior**?" I added the "Senior Senior" bit to be more exact.

She frowned, and even her wrinkles got wrinkles. "Do I look like a Frank?"

I didn't like to point out that she had a bit of a beard situation going on. Instead I said, "Do you know **Frank Davenport Senior Senior**?"

Her lips puckered up like a balloon knot and she nodded over to another wrinkly old person who was sitting in the corner.

And there he was, my Grandpa Frank.

CHAPTER 6

Don't eat food off people's bellies. It is not polite and a bit weird

The first time I saw my grandpa, he was asleep with three Bourbon biscuits balanced on his tummy. His faded Charlton Football Club shirt didn't quite cover his stomach and his silver belly hair was poking out, which made it look like he was smuggling a furry marmoset under his top. I thought it was a good sign that he was a Charlton supporter like me and Dad. On his bottom half he was wearing faded tracksuit bottoms, socks with flip-flops (which I didn't think was even possible) and, for some reason, a deerstalker hat – the type that Sherlock Holmes wears. I've never seen a stranger outfit before or since. And that includes the time Mum picked me up from school in a red-and-black ruffly dress which made her look like a flamenco dancer.

I was fairly certain I'd heard somewhere that if you wake up an old person and surprise them, they could drop dead from the shock. Because accidentally killing my grandpa probably wasn't what Grandma Nora had in mind when she asked me to look after him, I plonked myself down on a footstool next to him and waited for **Frank Senior Senior** to wake up naturally.

It was then that I noticed that he hadn't painted a picture on his canvas, but instead he'd written, in big black brush strokes, **I HAVE NOTHING TO BE HAPPY ABOUT.** While I admired his rebellious nature, it made me feel a bit sad for him. It also made me wonder what I would paint. I thought maybe a picture of me playing football or winning my reward. But for some reason that didn't make me feel particularly happy. Instead, a picture of me, Mum and Dad together with my new grandpa popped into my head. It was a nice thought.

Once I was done imagining that, I studied Grandpa

Frank's whiskery face and wondered what the first words we would say to each other might be. Whether he'd say something deep that I'd remember for ever.

After a few minutes of looking and pondering, I got a bit bored, because sitting next to an unconscious pensioner isn't exactly thrilling. And then I got a bit hungry, because I'd only had toast for my breakfast and, unlike Shreddies, toast does not keep hunger locked up until lunch. I was halfway through Grandpa

Frank's third Bourbon biscuit when he finally stirred.

He opened his eyes and looked down at the patch of brown crumbs on his Charlton top. By the way his huge fluffy eyebrows rammed together, I could tell he was wondering where his biccies had gone. I tried to gulp down the last of the evidence, but it was too late – he'd clocked what I'd done.

He said, "Well, I'll be blown. Have you been eating food off my belly?"

I HAVE NOTHING TO BE HAPPY ABOUT

I swallowed hard.

"Do I look like some sort of self-service buffet?" he went on in quite an angry voice.

So my new grandpa's first words to me weren't exactly deep or profound. And when he put it like that, it did make me question why I'd done it. Normal people don't eat food off people they don't know.

I think as I was a bit embarrassed, my first words weren't exactly the most heart-warming either, because I said, "Er, umm..."

"Er, umm" didn't exactly have a calming effect. He glared at me and said, quite loudly, "Admit it! You ate my biscuits!"

I didn't want to start off our relationship with a lie on top of the stomach-grazing, so I said, "I did eat your Bourbons, but only because I didn't want you to die."

He shuffled around in his chair so he was in a more upright position. "I'm only borderline diabetic. Three biscuits aren't going to kill me."

"I meant that I didn't want to wake you up and you drop dead from the shock, because I'm supposed to be looking after you, like Grandma Nora told me to. So I waited for you to wake up naturally, but you were taking ages, and I got a bit hungry, so that's why I ate the biscuits, and I would have asked but—"

I noticed his eyebrows were even more smooshed together now and he was looking at me with this really weird expression. He tilted his head to one side, readjusted his deerstalker and said, "Who did you say you were, biscuit-boy?"

I said, "Oh, I didn't say yet. I was busy explaining about the biscuits."

"I'm not interested in the biscuits any more. What I'm interested in is what you mean about being here to look after me. How do you know my Nora?"

"I don't know your Nora. I never met her and I can't now because she's dead. But she asked me to look after you..." I took a breath and looked him straight in the eyes. "Because I'm your grandson, Frank."

He didn't say anything, but he didn't need to, as his eyebrows were doing more than enough talking. They'd shot right to the top of his head and I thought they were saying, *A grandson – how delightful!*

It turns out I was wrong about that.

He leaned forward in his chair and pointed at me with a finger which was so thick it reminded me of a Cumberland sausage. "You're my grandson?"

"Yup, and you're my grandpa." I couldn't take my eyes off his sausage-finger. It was massive and it made me a bit nervous. My dream of having a new jolly grandpa wasn't going quite as smoothly as I had imagined.

He looked me up and down twice, like I was the most peculiar thing he'd ever seen – which was a bit rich, because he was the one wearing a hat with ear flaps. "My grandson?"

"That's right."

I held my hand out for a shake, but he didn't react, which was awkward. Instead, he jabbed his finger at me again. "*My grandson?*"

That was the third time he'd said it. Clearly, I'd broken my grandpa within minutes of meeting him. I'd overwhelmed his elderly brain. He'd short-circuited and was stuck on repeat, which – considering that the surprise reward was dependent on my looking after him well – was a bit of a blow.

Very slowly and loudly, I said, "Grandpa Frank, are you okay? Nod once for yes, twice for no."

He didn't nod AT ALL! Instead he said, "Are you simple or something, lad?"

I let out a long sigh. "That's a relief. For a moment there I thought you'd conked out."

"And why would you care if I'd conked out? Never shown any interest before."

I didn't tell him that was because I'd never had half a million quid and the chance of a mystery reward before, because that probably wouldn't have shown me in the best light. And I didn't explain that I had nothing else to do that summer, because I didn't want him to think I was just killing time with him. What I should have said was the truth – that I was actually quite happy to have a grandpa. But I didn't. Instead I said, "I didn't know about you until Grandma Nora died and left her will instructing me to look after you. And I think that is a very important, serious instruction."

He stared at me and said, "She did what? Why?"

"Good question. I would say you should ask her, but you can't because...well, you know...she's dead. But me looking after you was her last dying wish."

He looked upwards and said, "Now, why would you go and wish a thing like that, Nora?"

I followed his gaze, half expecting my dead step-grandmother to be stapled to the ceiling, but thankfully she wasn't.

"Anyway, I don't know *why* she did it, but she must've had a reason, don't you think?"

Grandpa Frank said, in a bit of an uncharitable tone, "She always had a reason for everything, that woman, but it doesn't mean it was a good reason."

"Hang on – I think she said something about you losing your factories."

His wrinkly chin dropped even further. "What do you mean, 'factories'?"

"I dunno – she wrote it. I would say you should ask her but—"

"Yes, I know, she's dead. Look, I don't need some kid looking after me."

"I'm not just some random kid, you know. I'm your grandson."

"And?"

"And I think that might mean something."

"I'm fine on my own."

"Are you fine? You seem a bit grumpy. I mean, look at your painting!"

I'd got him there. He couldn't really argue with a great big canvas that said **I HAVE NOTHING TO BE HAPPY ABOUT.**

He didn't respond, so I said, "And, if I'm honest, the way you're dressed, you look a bit…"

I hesitated.

"I look a bit what?"

I was going to say, *A bit like someone who doesn't own a mirror*, but I said, "Like someone who doesn't care."

He turned his head away and muttered, "That's exactly how I feel, since Nora passed. I've got nothing to care about."

I resisted the temptation to jump up and down and say, "Me! You could care about me!" because I'd only just met him, and it might have seemed a bit too needy. And besides, I didn't know why he couldn't work that one out for himself. But I did know things weren't going brilliantly. All I'd succeeded in doing was making him more miserable. That probably wasn't very reward-worthy.

I didn't say anything for a while. Then I turned the conversation to football, because, you know, sometimes that's the easiest thing to talk about. I nodded at his top. "I'm an Addicks supporter like you."

"You been to a game?"

I scooched my footstool closer to him.

"No, but Dad says he'll take me one day."

He picked up a newspaper from the coffee table and opened it out so I couldn't see his face. "And how is he – your father?"

At the time, I thought he'd said it like he didn't really care so I shrugged and just said, "He's alright."

"Ever talk about me?"

"Not really, I didn't know anything about you until the will thing."

He ruffled his newspaper and cleared his throat. "I see. Like that, is it?"

I shrugged again, not really sure what to say so I just said, "I guess. Don't you think it's a bit mad you two don't talk? Can't you both just...I dunno...move on?"

"Here's a piece of advice, kid – sometimes things don't go like you want. That's just life. Suck it up and trust only yourself. You hear that? Now get out of here. Go and play with your mates or something. I don't need you here pestering me."

I reckon he thought I'd be off after that. But as I didn't have any mates to play with, I wasn't going anywhere.

Besides, I don't quit easily and I knew what I had to do. It was time for **the sell**. I'd show him that I was offering him a once in a lifetime opportunity.

"Grandpa Frank, I've got almost **half a million quid** to spend on you to make sure you're properly looked after. Now, are you sure you want me to get out of here?"

The paper dropped down. He frowned a deep, deep frown. "Say that again, son."

See, money has a way of getting people's attention.

"I said, I've got almost **half a million quid** – well, **£462,000**, to be exact. That's how much Grandma Nora left me to look after you. You want a piece of that action or not?"

"**Half a million quid?!**" He dropped the newspaper into his lap. "You're having me on."

"I'm not."

"Nora doesn't have that sort of money."

"No, she doesn't. She's dead. But I have."

His chalky blue eyes ran over my face like he was trying to work out if I was fibbing or not.

"**Half a million quid?**"

"Pretty much."

"**Half a million quid?**"

"Well, almost. It's a few thousand short."

"**HALF A MILLION QUID!**"

He was stuck on repeat again. I was beginning to think that this time I really had broken him, but then he leaped to his flip-flopped feet (which was a bit of a surprise because I had not considered him the leaping sort) and said, "Well, punch me in the belly and call me Clara."

"You want me to punch you *where* and call you *what*?"

He didn't say anything for a moment, but I could tell he was thinking.

Then he pointed at me with his Cumberland again. "First thing you need to do, Franky boy, is get yourself down the corner shop and pick me up a packet of Bourbons." He readjusted his hat and then, with no warning, marched out of the lounge.

I called after him, "Clara – I mean, Grandpa – where are you going? I'm supposed to be looking after you. We have things we need to discuss."

He kept on walking but shouted over his shoulder, "Bourbons first, moneybags, then we can talk about how this is going to work."

I can't say our first meeting went exactly how I'd envisioned it. I had a sense that Grandpa Frank was going to be more trouble to look after than I'd originally thought. But I guess even if I *had* known, I would still have tried anyway. The chance of a mystery reward was way too tempting – and so was the chance of having my own real-life grandpa.

Electrocuting old people is frowned upon

I wasn't sure if Grandpa Frank was serious about the biscuits, but I popped round to the corner shop and picked some up anyway. When I got back, Stephen, the guy I'd met at reception, was in the middle of a heated phone discussion about what he was having for his tea. He held up his hand for me to wait and I pretended not to listen to him tell some guy called Tyronne that mushrooms were in fact the work of the devil.

When he had finished, he asked what I thought of mushrooms. I shrugged, "I guess of all the fungi, they're my favourite."

Stephen laughed. "I suppose they are better than

athlete's foot. Just." Then he nodded to a corridor off to the right. "Come on, I'll show you to your grandpa's room."

On the way he clocked the packet of Bourbons under my arm. "Don't you let him eat the whole lot of those. I shudder to think about your grandpa's blood sugar levels."

"I'll try not to."

We came to a stop outside a door with Davenport written on a laminated sign and he said, "Here we are, you have fun now, you hear?" Then made his way back to reception.

I knocked on the door and shouted, "Biscuit delivery."

"You took your own sweet time," he called out. "What did you do, bake them yourself?"

I took that to mean I could go in. I pushed the door open to find him sitting on his bed with a suitcase by his feet, which were now in trainers and not flip-flops. He was also wearing a suit jacket over his football top. But still the deerstalker. Someone really needed to have a word with him about that.

"You going somewhere?"

"You'd better believe it. I'm not sticking around this dump with **£462,000** to my name." He gestured at me to give him the biscuits. "Hand them over, I'll eat them on the cab ride to the airport."

I pulled them away from him. He was as bad as Mum and Dad. "What do you mean, to your name? That money is mine."

"To spend on me."

"No, to look after you in your final years."

"Could be *your* final year if you don't do as I say."

I folded my arms. I wasn't going to be threatened by an old guy in questionable headgear. "Don't be difficult, I'm here to help you."

"I'll tell you what, I'll make it easy for you. The best way you can help me is to get me a nice little villa on the Costa del Sol."

"What is it with old people and the Costa del Sol? That's where my other grandparents live."

"Lucky them. I bet it would be perfect. Me, by myself, nobody else. Heaven."

"I don't think that's what Grandma Nora meant AT ALL."

"You never met her, so how would you know? Sun, sea, sand and solitude – that's all I want before I kick the bucket."

"Before you what?"

"You know – before I'm put to bed with a shovel, before I go belly up, before I assume room temperature."

I looked at him blankly.

"Before I die, lad. Send me off to Spain and you'll have looked after me very well indeed."

"No can do, I'm afraid, Grandpa. I need to oversee your care. That's what the will says." I wasn't a hundred per cent sure about that, but he hadn't seen it, and neither had I, so I thought I was on safe enough ground.

I pulled out my phone, opened the notes section and sat on the armchair in the corner of the room. "So, tell me. What does an old person like you need to live?"

"I told you, the four S's – sun, sea, sand and solitude. Actually, you can forget the sand – it has a habit of getting stuck in my bum wrinkles."

I ignored that harrowing image and moved on. "If you're not going to give me any proper help, I'm going to google it." I typed **What do old people need** into the search engine and showed him the results. "It says right here, look – care, security, company and love."

Grandpa Frank pulled a face. "What a load of old bunkum."

I had to agree. It wasn't exactly practical. There was a pop-up advert that gave me an idea though. "How about slippers? Would you like some slippers?"

"Go steady there, wouldn't want you blowing all your cash at once."

Stephen, the man from reception, poked his head around the door. He had a massive smile on his face and I noticed his chipped tooth again. "And how are the Davenport men doing? Are you getting on famously?"

Suddenly the smile was gone, and he stepped into the room with his arms folded over his belly and glared at Grandpa Frank. "You want to tell me why you've got that suitcase packed again, Mr Davenport? Not planning another one of your breakouts?"

Grandpa Frank puffed up his chest. "Nothing keeping me here – I can go if I like. Can't keep me prisoner."

"Breakouts?" I looked at Grandpa, wide-eyed. "You escaped from here?"

Stephen answered for him. "Yes, fourteen times since Mrs Davenport passed. Understandably, after almost ten years of living here together, Mr Davenport has found it difficult being here without her, but we're working on that."

This wasn't good news. I couldn't have Grandpa doing a runner when I was supposed to be doing reward-worthy care-giving on him. "Well, you're going to have to make sure he doesn't get out again."

"I can go where I please. I'm a free man."

Frankly, he needed to get rid of that sort of attitude. He wasn't a free man, he was **my grandpa** and he belonged to me now. He was my ticket to a possibly excellent reward.

"Isn't there some sort of lock system?" I looked around the room. "This place doesn't seem very secure. I mean, there aren't even bars on the windows. No wonder he was able to escape."

"I'm not sure that a prison-vibe is the sort of atmosphere Autumnal Leaves is going for," Stephen said.

"Could have fooled me," Grandpa muttered.

"Look, I've literally just googled it, security is one of the things old people need. Maybe we could set up some electrified perimeter fence to keep Grandpa and the rest of them in?"

Stephen laughed like he thought I was joking. "You want nuked nonagenarians scattered all over the place?"

"Huh?"

"You want to electrocute ninety year olds?" he explained.

I guessed not. "Or maybe you could attach one of those ankle tags or a tracking device to him, so if he tries anything we know where he is? I don't care how much it costs. I'm good for the money."

Stephen and Grandpa both looked at me. Neither of them blinked for what seemed like ages.

Eventually Stephen said, "You want to electronically chip your grandpa?"

I shrugged. "It's not the worst idea in the world. I don't want him running away."

Stephen sounded quite put out when he said, "He's not some kind of pet."

What was wrong with everybody? Had I *said* he was some kind of pet? "Look, Stephen, I've got instructions to look after my grandpa and I take that very seriously."

"So. Do. I." Stephen said that quite forcefully. Then he picked up Grandpa Frank's suitcase and opened it up. Very gently, he said, "Here, Mr Davenport, let me help you unpack," and started taking things out and putting them back into Grandpa's cupboards. While he was doing this, he said to me, in a much calmer voice, "The thing is, young Frank, Mr Davenport's never gone long. He always comes back, don't you, Mr Davenport?"

Grandpa Frank let out a long sad sigh and looked out the window. I might have been wrong, but his eyes looked a little bit watery. Then he said something so quietly that only my very young and functioning ears could hear it. He said, "That's because I've nowhere else to go."

And I thought, **BRILLIANT!**

If he wasn't going anywhere, I could care for him as instructed. The reward, whatever it was – and I was beginning to think it was probably unbelievable amounts of cash – was as good as mine. And so, hopefully, was he.

I just needed to figure out how to do caring beyond supplying slippers. And that was going to require some more in-depth research on my good friend, Google.

CHAPTER 8

Beware of falling into
a YouTube hole

That very same evening, after I'd had my tea – which Mum had claimed was lasagne and Dad had described as cheesy-tomatoey slop – I set about finding out all there was to know about grandparent maintenance.

Mum and Dad had tried to get me to stay and talk to them about *"this nonsense of looking after Grandpa Frank"*. I didn't tell them I'd been to see him because I'm bright enough to know it wouldn't have gone down well. They started banging on about how he was a difficult man and that I was just a kid and how it was a ridiculous situation. To be honest, I tuned out and said nothing until they'd finished.

Then I said, "Can I go now?"

Mum did a big sigh and said, "Fine."

And I scarpered upstairs to my computer as quick as my legs could take me.

I love the internet. It can tell you everything you want to know – as long as you know what to put into Google. I *thought* I knew what to put into Google, but it turns out that when you type **How to care for a really old person in a really excellent reward-winning way**, you get all sorts of random stuff.

Now, I hold my hands up – I quickly lost sight of what I was supposed to be doing. Somehow, after I'd watched a video on Zimmer-frame maintenance, I ended up watching a Zimmer-frame race between three elderly ladies, which got surprisingly physical, truth be told. That video then took me to a video about how to maintain healthy bones – spoiler alert, it's lots of calcium. And then I ended up watching someone called Betty teaching me how to make my own purple hair dye, the lilac-y type that old women seem to like. I'd forgotten all about the grandfather-care advice I was supposed to be searching for and fallen into a very deep YouTube hole. It was only when Dad left in a hurry around nine o'clock that I snapped out of the video vortex.

He didn't make the quietest of exits. I looked out my bedroom window and watched Mum follow him out the front door and start attacking him under a street light with the bunch of flowers he'd bought her. He was apologizing, saying he'd "sort it". At the time I thought the *it* he was talking about was probably me and the inheritance money. I didn't stop to think that it could be something else. Really, the fact that he'd bought her flowers should have been a clue that he'd got himself into trouble again. But I guess we all get wrapped up in ourselves sometimes.

Anyway, Mum stomped back inside, shouting, "You'd better sort this, Frank, or it will be me you'll be scared of." And then she slammed the front door.

I watched Dad a little longer. He must have been annoyed because he kicked a wheelie bin and ended up apologizing to scary-looking Bob from next door. Once Bob had backed down, Dad skulked off with his head bowed and his hands stuck in his pockets. I reckoned he'd be off down the pub.

I closed my curtains and flopped down onto my bed and, I admit it, I started to feel a bit sorry for myself. We weren't exactly a picture of a happy family. I hated that no one seemed to be getting on. My parents were fighting with each other and I could tell they were annoyed at me. I didn't understand why they couldn't just let me have my money and let me look after Grandpa Frank like I wanted to.

The heavy feeling I sometimes get in my tummy was back and, even though I was trying to ignore them, I could feel prickles at the back of my eyes.

I wasn't going to cry though. Wallowing isn't good for anybody. And besides, Dad always said Davenport men don't cry and I believed him. So, instead of the waterworks, I gave myself a full-body shake, took a deep breath and thought about something else – well, somebody else. Grandpa Frank.

I sat back at my computer and said out loud, "No more YouTube," so I knew I meant it, and then I told myself to think...

To think carefully about what I wanted to put into Google.

To think carefully about what I wanted to do for Grandpa Frank.

To maybe even think about what *he* wanted. What had he said? That all he wanted to do before he kicked the bucket was to live in Spain in solitude?

That sounded rubbish. I couldn't believe that anyone would want to spend their last days on their own doing nothing. No one wants to be on their own. If I was old, I'd want to make the most of my time. Do everything I could before it was too late. Find something that would make me happy.

I remembered Grandpa's grumpy painting: **I HAVE NOTHING TO BE HAPPY ABOUT**. And that's when an idea came to me. Suddenly, caring for Grandpa Frank meant only one thing – helping him to live his best life ever. I'd give him something – more than one something, to paint on that blank canvas.

I typed in **All the things you should do before you kick the bucket**.

And guess what?

The results were waaaaay more interesting than any Zimmer-frame race I've ever seen.

I leaned back in my chair, gave my knuckles a satisfying crack and said out loud – because I just *knew* it was one of *those* moments – "This is going to be totally epic."

It's funny to think now that this was where it all started. When I first saw the words **The Bucket List**.

Not all animals
can be ridden

The next morning was the second day of the summer holidays and even though I hadn't had much sleep, I wasn't tired – I was very motivated. And that was because I had spent most of the night coming up with a list of activities to help Grandpa enjoy his last few years on this planet. What could be more caring than that?

Sure, I wasn't certain that Grandpa Frank would be super pumped about all of them, but I reckoned all I had to do was **sell** it to him in the right way.

I was munching through my Shreddies, hoping they'd keep hunger at bay until lunch to avoid any awkward biscuit situations, when Mum walked into the room in a bright pink suit and with her hair all piled on top of her head, which made it look like a croissant. She looked a bit fancy for a shift at Grigsby's, so I said, "It's Sunday, I thought you were working today?"

She said, "I've swapped with Elaine – she's doing the early, I'm doing the late." Then she paused before saying, "Frank, my love..." in a way that made me realize she was going to spring something on me that I wouldn't like.

I just went, "Uh huh?" and kept spooning in my pillows of wheat.

She perched on the breakfast stool next to me. "Sweetheart, you need to know that your father and I are going to speak to some lawyer friend of his about the money."

I didn't even look at her, just kept shovelling in the Shreddies until I had so many in my mouth that I wouldn't have been able to speak even if I'd wanted to. I continued to angry-chomp them while she spoke.

"Darling, it would be obvious to a goldfish that there's been a monumental mistake and, I'm sorry, but we would not be responsible parents if we let you keep that amount of money or let you attempt to look after your grandpa."

I think I must have rolled my eyes or something because then she said, "Don't you disrespect me with that face of yours, Frank John Davenport. I'm only trying to do what is best for you and him."

I didn't say anything, *couldn't* say anything – not just because of all the Shreddies, but because I knew if I did say, *I don't think someone who looks like they've got a pastry stuck to their head knows what's best*, I would not get a good reaction. But I did think, *You try and take my money, lady. Just you try.* And I sat there and silently fumed.

Mum did not seem to pick up on the atmosphere in the room – probably because it was just inside me – and she gave me a kiss on top of my head, which I didn't want. Then she shouted at the ceiling, "FRANK, are you ready?" in a volume that was not at all considerate of how close she was to me.

Dad walked through the door, his hair sticking out at all angles, and said, "You bellowed?" He looked a bit grey around the edges – he was probably tired from having been out so late the night before.

"We're going to miss the appointment." Mum then stuck her hands on her hips and looked him up and down. She did not look delighted by what she saw. "Could you smarten yourself up a bit?"

Dad tried to stuff his T-shirt into his jeans and flatten his hair down with his hands. Mum sighed and shook her head. "You'll have to do." Then she turned to me and said, "We won't be too long. You stay here and play on your computer games until we get back. If you need us, then phone, understand?"

I grunted, because I was not in the mood to make agreements with the very woman who was trying to swindle me out of my riches.

She swooshed out of the kitchen, her high heels clacking on the tiles, and threw a casual, "Bye, kiddo," over her shoulder like she wasn't about to try and ruin everything for me. Dad grabbed a brown-looking banana from the fruit bowl, pretended to shoot me with it and said, "This banana's gone bad," before disappearing out of the door after her, which annoyed me even more because I didn't get a chance to tell him that it was a terrible joke.

I decided to sit and silently fume for a good few minutes more. Turns out, I'm pretty good at silently fuming. Frankly, I could have gone on for ages, but I was distracted from my fumification when I heard the doorbell ring. It was one of the neighbours bringing our post which had accidentally gone in their letter box the day before. Amongst the bills were two official-looking letters addressed to me. I tore them open. In one was a bank card. In the other was a letter with a weird scratch-off panel that turned out to be the PIN – a four-digit number that was the code to getting my hands on all that cash.

I punched my fist in the air and shouted, "Get in!"

Operation Grandpa Frank's Great Big Bucket List was all systems go! Mum and Dad could meet whatever lawyers they wanted, I was the one with the bank card! A bank card that I was going to make sure Mum and Dad knew nothing about.

I pulled my phone out of my pocket and googled a number for a taxi to take me to Autumnal Leaves.

But then I had a better idea and I dialled a different number. As Dad says, there's no point in having money if you're not going to spend it.

A woman came on the end of the phone. "East London Farm Zoo."

I got straight to business. "Hi, how much would it cost to hire a camel to take me from Lewisham to Bromley?"

She said, "Excuse me?"

I didn't know what she had done but I thought it was best to be polite, so I said, "You're excused."

"No, I mean did you actually ask about hiring a camel?"

"Yes. Do you have any?"

"No." She was a bit abrupt when she dropped that disappointing bombshell.

I decided to be the bigger person and stay dead

polite. "Could you possibly tell me what animals you do have?"

I think my politeness helped her regain some professionalism because she said, "I guess...well, we have goats—"

"No." Too small.

"Sheep—"

"No." Also too small.

"Alpaca—"

"Bingo. How much to hire an alpaca to take me from Lewisham to Bromley?"

"You can't ride an alpaca!"

"How do you know? I might be excellent at it."

"You can't ride an alpaca because they're too small."

"Are they? I thought they were similar to horses in size. The ones I've seen are quite big and fluffy. They definitely look rideable."

"I reckon you'd need about three alpaca to equal one horse. They are actually quite skinny under all that fur. Definitely not big enough to be ridden."

"Really?"

"Yes, really. Do you want a squashed alpaca? Is that what you want?"

She was clearly bonkers. Nobody wants a squashed alpaca. "I just want to use some of my money to get to my grandpa's old people's home in a really cool way. Do you have llamas and, if so, are they big enough to be ridden?"

I thought it was a reasonable question, but she hung up after that.

I ended up hiring a limo. Which was cool, but certainly not camel or alpaca levels of cool.

When the driver showed up at mine, my stomach did this flippety-flopping thing, which I put down to the excitement that comes with luxury travel. But thinking about it now, I guess I was also pretty nervous. I really wanted Grandpa Frank to have a good time.

And I really wanted him to like me.

CHAPTER 10

You can get anybody to do what you want – you've just got to sell it well

For a while, it did feel pretty awesome to be driven by limo. I made the driver go really slowly when we went by the park so Tyler Scott and the other kids could see me. I stood up so I was half through the sunroof and waved. Their jaws dropped to their ankles which made me laugh for a bit. But when I dropped back down into the car, I realized I was laughing to myself and I suddenly didn't feel so great. I was pleased that it wasn't too long before we arrived at Autumnal Leaves.

I pushed my way through the double doors and went up to reception. The first things I noticed were two giant canvases hanging up behind the desk. One was the weird pterodactyl painting and the other was the ant/horse painting that I'd seen the old ladies painting the day before. Unsurprisingly, Grandpa Frank's **I HAVE NOTHING TO BE HAPPY ABOUT** had not made the wall.

Stephen was dusting the fake plastic plants but stopped when he saw me and waved very enthusiastically with his feather duster. "You're back! I'm so pleased to see you and I'm sure Mr Davenport will be too. Even if he doesn't show it on the outside."

"He's going to be delighted when I tell him what I've got planned." I probably sounded a bit overconfident when I said that, but it was difficult not to, because I was. Grandpa Frank couldn't not be delighted.

Stephen smiled. "I'm sure he will. He's in his room; do you remember the way?"

I nodded.

"Well you go straight in. But, just to warn you, he's had a few fuzzy moments this morning. Nothing to worry about though."

"What do you mean, fuzzy?" I got the impression he didn't mean like a bear.

"A bit forgetful, that's all." He put his non-duster-holding hand on my shoulder and said gently, "Do try and be patient with him."

"I can do that. I am a very patient person."

Stephen smiled and said, "I can tell that. You seem like a great grandson."

That made me blush, but I kind of liked being called a great grandson. I hadn't been called a great *anything* for ages.

I was still enjoying the compliment when suddenly Stephen rammed his duster right under my nostrils. "But no more talk of electrocuting my residents with three-metre-high perimeter fences, okay?"

"Okay...but I still don't think it was a *terrible* idea. I wasn't suggesting thousands and thousands of volts, more like a quick buzz as a deterrent."

Stephen stared at me. "No electric fences. Say it."

"Fine. No electric fences."

"Off you go, have fun with Mr Davenport."

I wandered down the corridor to Grandpa Frank's room, knocked on his door and said, "It's me."

He shouted back, "Not today, thanks."

I opened the door anyway.

He was wearing exactly what he'd been wearing the day before. Including the deerstalker. He said, "What are you doing here? Does your mother know you're here?"

I said, "Not exactly." Then, because Grandpa Frank was sitting in his armchair, I flopped down on the bed. "But it's fine. She won't even notice I'm gone."

"That woman notices everything. Where's your brother Vinny? Isn't he supposed to be looking after you?"

"I look after myself. Besides, I don't have a brother Vinny." It took me a moment, but then I realized something. "Hey, wait a minute...do you mean *Uncle* Vinny who lives in Ireland and works the waltzers? Do you think I'm *my dad*? I'm Frank, your *grandson*." I laughed.

Grandpa Frank looked at me and I noticed a sudden flicker of recognition in his eyes. "Of course I know you're my grandson. It's your fault for coming in here, looking like *him*, trying to confuse me. *On purpose.*"

It wasn't my fault, but he looked a bit angry – you know, the sort of angry you get when you think you've embarrassed yourself – so I didn't point it out. Instead, I said, "I'm sorry you think that," which is not a real apology because I wasn't admitting any fault on my part. I think I learned that from Dad.

Anyway, it seemed to do the trick, because he didn't look quite so cross, but his shoulders did this sad slumpy thing. It made him look very small and old and I didn't like him looking like that one bit, so I said, "Hey, cheer up, it's no biggie," because I really thought it wasn't.

I realize now, of course, how wrong I was about that. It's funny how, sometimes, the smallest things that you hardly notice turn out to be the biggest.

I cleared my throat, keen to get going with my plan. "Anyway, on to today's business." I quite liked how I sounded when I said that – like a very professional grandfather-carer.

Grandpa Frank leaned forward in his armchair and arched one very curious, furry eyebrow. "Today's business?"

From my back pocket I took out the piece of paper where I'd written my own **Bucket List** and unfolded it in a dramatic fashion.

"Here we go," Grandpa Frank muttered.

"As your appointed carer, I'm here to help you make the most of the time you have left."

He splutter-laughed as he said, "What are you, some sort of angel of death?"

I hadn't thought of it like that, but I have to say, I wasn't completely against the comparison. It made me sound important. "Yeah, if you like, and to help you live your best life, I've drawn up a **Bucket List** for you—"

"You've gone and done what?"

"A **Bucket List**! *You know*, a list of all the things you should do before you go for – what was it you said? – your final nap in the dirt." I gave him a huge triumphant grin, because I was feeling very triumphant.

He said, "Well, pull my hair and whistle up my nose. I don't believe what my ears are telling me." Which made me think he was *very* impressed by my efforts.

"We should get going," I continued. "There's quite a lot of things we need to do and, no offence, Grandpa, you haven't got that long to do them."

He gave me the same weird look as when he'd realized I'd eaten biscuits off his belly.

"This is the most ridiculous thing I've ever heard. *Live my best life?* You sound like some kind of motivational speaker and no real person should sound like one of those. And especially not a Davenport. You'll have me in a leotard doing yoga and going '*Ommm*' before I know it."

It wasn't the reaction I'd hoped for, but it was the one I'd expected. If he was anything like Dad, he wouldn't be the sort for lunging in Lycra, but Grandpa Frank was lucky because that wasn't what I had in mind (at that point anyway). I grinned at him even wider and said, "That's not a strong *no* though, is it?"

He slumped back even further in his chair and glared at me some more. "It's not a yes either."

Time for **the sell**. Again. "What else have you got to do?"

"Nothing. And I don't see anything wrong with that."

"And I don't see anything right about that either." I'd been staring at a summer holiday full of a whole load of *nothing* before I'd made my **Bucket List** plan. There was no way it wasn't happening. "Don't you have goals?

Things you want to do? You don't want to end up with a whole bunch of regrets, do you?"

"And this is where we differ. My goal is to do not very much and do it on my own. And as for regrets, it's too late to worry about those. Now, if you don't mind, I'd like to take a nap."

Like all good salesmen, I'd prepared for this kind of response. I needed to show him I had something he wanted. "Alright, Grandpa, how's about after you've completed your **Bucket List** I'll sort you out with your own villa in the Costa del Sunshine?"

He sat up a little straighter when I said that and stared at me. "You telling the truth? A villa in Spain?"

"I give you my word." There was no way he'd want to disappear to Spain once I started caring for him.

I let him think about it for a moment. Eventually he sighed and said, "I'm going to live to regret this."

"But at least you'll be living, Grandpa."

He exhaled very slowly, then said, "What did I say about motivational quotes?"

"Not to say them."

I thought I might have blown it, but then he held out

his big spade-like hand and I shook it. It was warmer and softer than I had expected it to be.

"You have made an excellent decision," I told him.

He looked up at the ceiling and sighed again. "What's on this list of yours then?"

I looked back at my piece of paper. I'd intended to start with the very first one, but something told me it would be better to ease Grandpa Frank in gently. Cage diving with a great white shark could wait for a week or two. It was important that I chose the exact right thing to get off to an excellent start and not scare him away. And we couldn't go to watch the Addicks play as it wasn't the footie season...

"Aha! Got it. You're going to love this."

"I doubt it."

I said, "That's the spirit, Grandpa," but I was being sarcastic. "How do you feel about a **hot-air balloon ride**?"

"A hot-air balloon ride?" The way he said it you would have thought I'd suggested having his liver removed through his armpit.

It was like he already knew it would end in disaster.

CHAPTER 11

Sometimes people say they're smashing when they're not

I was thinking about ordering another stretch limo so I could get home before Mum, when Stephen poked his head into Grandpa Frank's bedroom.

"There's a man outside who says he's your father. He's come to pick you up."

That wasn't brilliant news. "How did he know I was here?"

Stephen frowned. "How am I supposed to know that?"

I noticed Grandpa Frank craning his neck to look out the window.

"Do you want to come and say hi?"

He picked up the newspaper that was lying on his bedside table and made a show of opening it out in front of his face. "If your father wants to speak to me, he knows where I am."

"The stuff that happened between you went on ages ago. Can't you just put it all behind you? Come on! He's just outside. I'm sure he'd be pleased to see you." I wasn't a hundred per cent sure that was the honest truth, but it was mad that they weren't talking. Maybe this was a chance for them to make amends.

Grandpa Frank didn't seem to think so though. "He's got legs. If he wants to see me, he can use them. I'm busy reading my paper."

"I don't think you're actually reading your newspaper."

"What do you think I'm doing with it then? Using it to wipe my backside?"

"I think you're hiding behind it. Or using it as a metaphorical barrier to maintain distance between us."

Now, to be honest, I don't have a clue what I said there. A teacher at one of the schools I went to – I don't remember her name, but I do remember her big concerned eyeballs – called me in once to talk about "how things were at home". I wasn't particularly interested in listening to what she had to say, so while she blathered on about support being there if I needed it, I picked up a school newsletter and pretended to read it – which is when she mentioned the metaphorical barrier thing.

Stephen said, "Ooh, he's got you there, Mr Davenport."

Grandpa Frank turned a page and said, "I'm not moving, and I will not cave to pressure," in a way that made me know his flip-flopped feet weren't going anywhere.

"Fine. I'll ask Dad if he wants to pop up. If not, I'll see you tomorrow for the first activity on our **Bucket List**."

He turned another page. "Do what you want."

I darted out the door, then dashed back and said, "I'm excited to be caring for you, Grandpa Frank. Are you excited?"

He didn't look out from behind the newspaper and said, in a very deadpan voice, "I'm ecstatic." He obviously wanted me to *think* he wasn't excited, when he actually was. After all, who wouldn't be excited about a trip in a hot-air balloon?

"Okay, see you tomorrow then. You won't regret it!"

When I got outside, I had been planning to grill Dad about how him and Mum had got on at the solicitors, but I forgot about that because he was in a car I'd never seen before. The bonnet was a different colour to the rest of the bodywork, and it smelled of stale cigarettes.

He leaned out the window. "Alright, son? Get in."

"Where did you get this?"

"Borrowed it from a mate."

I never like it when Dad uses the word *borrowed*. I think it has a slightly different meaning for him.

I climbed in the passenger seat. "How did you know I was here? Am I in trouble? Does Mum know?"

"Let's say it was an educated guess. And no, you're not in trouble. When I was your age, I was always off getting up to stuff." He turned the key in the ignition. "And your mum has a way of finding out everything – you'd do well to remember that."

"Where is she?"

"At work – she's on the late shift."

"You don't want to come in and say hi to your dad before we go? I think he'd like to see you."

Dad turned to look at me. "He said that, did he?"

I couldn't lie. "Not in so many words, but I'm sure he would."

Dad looked at the front entrance and for a moment I thought he might go in...but then he slid the car into reverse. "Some other time perhaps, son. In a bit of a rush."

I noticed then that he looked a bit agitated – panicky even – so I said, "Everything alright?"

He gave me his usual big smile – the same smile he gave me any time one of his money-making schemes backfired. "Everything's smashing."

I mustn't have looked convinced because he rubbed my hair and said, "Don't look at me with your face hanging out like that. You know you don't need to worry about your old man."

I nodded, but I didn't know that. I didn't know that at all. Dad had a history of getting himself into tricky situations. It's hard not to worry about someone when they do that.

He kept the engine running when we pulled up outside our house.

"Are you not coming in?"

"I've got some business to attend to."

At the time, I thought "some business" was probably to do with my money, so I told him, in a bit of a stroppy manner, that I'd be alright on my own. Which was the truth – I was used to it.

"Look, no hard feelings about the money, hey, son? It's just, you know, it's best all round if your mum and I take control of it. And maybe you should knock these visits to your grandpa's on the head, hey?"

Before I could tell him that wouldn't be happening, his phone bleeped and a message popped up. He swiped it away before I had a chance to read it, but I didn't miss the fact that all the colour drained from his face.

"Everything okay, Dad?"

He smiled his big fake smile again, but he couldn't look me in the eye when he said, "Like I said, everything's smashing. Gotta go, son. Places to be, people to see, money to make."

I slammed the door so he'd know I wasn't happy. I thought he might say something about that, but he didn't. He just drove out of our estate with this big black cloud of smoke billowing out of his exhaust.

Because the slamming of the car door hadn't been quite enough to get my crossness out, I also slammed the front door. And because I didn't want to think about what Dad was up to, I went and angry-ate a whole twelve-pack of Babybel and a tub of Mum's posh yoghurt from the fridge. When she got home later that evening, she was in one of her chatty moods, but I didn't want to talk to her about how annoying it is when people don't have their coupons ready by the time they get to the checkout. I just wanted to be on my own. So I turned down her offer to heat up one of her cottage pies – to be honest, it hadn't been lovely the first time around. Instead, I took a cheese toastie and a glass of milk up to my room and concentrated on being an excellent reward-winning carer for Grandpa Frank.

I booked a hot-air balloon flight for the following morning. Luckily, there'd been a cancellation and I was able to persuade Dave, the hot-air balloon man, to squeeze us in. According to Balloon Dave, the weather looked a bit breezy, but after I offered him another hundred quid as a bribe, he thought the conditions would be good enough to go up. And because I thought he was an expert, I believed him.

CHAPTER 12

Always check the back door of a minibus before driving off

Over breakfast the next morning, when Mum and Dad asked what I was going to do with myself for the day, I just told them I was off for a kickabout in the park with some mates. If they'd paid more attention to the fact that I don't have any, they might have asked some more questions. But Mum just told me to have fun and stay safe and to phone if I needed anything and Dad told me to make sure I practised with my left foot too.

I waited for Mum to go to work at the supermarket and for Dad to go wherever he goes for work and then I ordered a regular taxi to take me to Autumnal Leaves.

I didn't want to take the shine off the hot-air balloon ride later by starting the day riding something awesome like a camel. I had to get the driver to take me to five different cashpoints, because they only let you take out two hundred pounds each time and I needed a fair amount of cash to pay Balloon Dave. I think the driver might have been getting a bit too interested in what I was up to, but I tipped him a fiver and gave him one of my Match Attack cards and he stopped asking questions.

When I arrived at Autumnal Leaves, I had a grand in my pocket, but I was feeling like a million quid.

Grandpa Frank must have been a bit excited, because he'd put on a tie over his football top. When I said, "Nice of you to dress up special," he didn't accept the compliment like a normal person.

Instead, he turned on me and said, "Why do you insist on wearing those ridiculous trousers that make your legs look like sticks of liquorice?"

I looked down at my skinny jeans. "Everyone wears them like this. It's the fashion."

Grandpa shook his head. "It's a wonder they haven't cut off the circulation to your brain."

"This is what we're doing, is it? I stand here and you take the mickey and then I pay for you to have an experience of a lifetime."

He looked at me steadily. "That's exactly what we seem to be doing, yes."

I was about to feel very annoyed with him, but then I noticed a slight smile at the edge of his mouth. It reminded me a bit of Dad, and I found myself smiling right back.

"Right," he said. "Shall we get this ordeal over with?"

It was at this point that I realized I hadn't actually thought of a way of getting us to the take-off field, which was a fair distance out of town. Which, considering I'd been so transport-focused recently, was a surprising omission on my part.

I phoned a load of taxi companies, but nobody had anything for over an hour. I then tried ringing for a helicopter, but according to the man I spoke to, they don't work like Uber.

When Grandpa Frank had finished blaming my lack of foresight on my too-tight jeans limiting the oxygen supply to my brain, he came up with what – on the face of it – seemed like a brilliant idea.

"Autumnal Leaves has a minibus," he announced. "And I have a driving licence."

Neither of these statements were lies. It just turned out that his driving licence had expired twelve years earlier and the Autumnal Leaves minibus was about a hundred years older than its oldest resident. But I didn't think to ask about the bus's road-worthiness, or Grandpa's for that matter, because all I was thinking about was hot-air ballooning. (I definitely considered their road-worthiness later though, when we were travelling at twenty-six miles an hour in a cloud of black smoke down the dual carriageway. But by then there was not much I could do about it.)

Anyway, Grandpa Frank seemed to think Stephen would frown on us borrowing the minibus, so he made me stand guard and keep watch while he ducked around the back of the reception desk, opened a drawer and pulled out a bunch of keys. He had this mischievous look in his eyes, which made me realize exactly where Dad got his slightly-less-than-law-abiding tendencies from.

We ran to the side of the building where the minibus was parked and jumped in. Grandpa turned on the ignition and the engine spluttered. Even though neither of us were mechanics, we both said, "That doesn't sound very good."

After a fifteen-point turn, the knocking over of the Autumnal Leaves sign and the creation of a small dink in the front of the minibus, Grandpa slammed his foot down on the accelerator and we were off.

At least we thought we were off.

We heard the wailing at the same time. Grandpa Frank slammed the brakes on and we looked behind us to see that the back doors of the minibus were wide open.

Grandpa was out of his seat in a flash. "Smack me round the face with a side of salmon! That was Brenda! She must have been in the back!"

"What?" I said. "Why do they keep her in the minibus?"

"The silly trout has just rolled out the back doors!"

Brenda, it turned out, was the Autumnal Leaves resident I'd met before. The one in the wheelchair with the beard situation.

I ran to the back of the bus and found Grandpa Frank trying to wheel her back on board. "What are you doing?"

"She's involved now. She's seen too much. She's going to have to come with us."

I said, "What?"

Brenda said, "What?"

Grandpa said, "Are you going to help me load her back on, or stand there looking gormless?"

All I could say was, "*What?*" again.

Brenda said, "Are you taking me to my acupuncture appointment?"

Grandpa Frank ignored that and said, "If we're going to make that hot-air balloon flight, Brenda's going to have to come too. We can't have her going inside, shouting her mouth off about us stealing the minibus."

"I thought we were borrowing it!"

"Same thing." It seemed Grandpa had the same outlook on borrowing as Dad.

"We can't take Brenda hostage. We could go to prison if she complains."

Grandpa and I both looked at Brenda and he said, "You going to complain?"

She straightened her blouse and said, "It certainly sounds better than having needles stuck into me. I've always wanted to go on a hot-air balloon flight. It's on my bucket list, actually."

Grandpa grabbed hold of the handles of the wheelchair again. "Mine too, apparently."

Grandpa managed to find the button that lowered the ramp and we rolled Brenda back up it and onto the minibus. I slammed the back doors – this time making sure they were properly shut – and we drove off.

It wasn't the ideal start to **Grandpa Frank's Great Big Bucket List**, but if Brenda was the only bump in the road, I was still confident we'd have an awesome time.

I just didn't realize how much chaos one elderly woman in a wheelchair could wreak.

CHAPTER 13

Do your research before you get into a hot-air balloon

I'd never been so pleased to arrive at a destination – not because I was excited about the hot-air ballooning (although I was), but more because I was pleased Grandpa Frank had managed not to kill us all on the A20. That would have been a very disappointing start to the **Bucket List**. I never thought I'd find a driver worse than both of my parents, but there you go.

Balloon Dave greeted us, wafting away the cloud of minibus exhaust smoke with his massive hands. "You must be Frank," he said, shaking my hand. He had what Dad would call a decent handshake, because it made me feel like my finger bones might shatter.

He helped me unload Brenda, who seemed to be increasingly chuffed about her impromptu day out. "Now," he said, "it might seem a tad blowy, but we should still be fine to go up. I'm keen to get the balloon in the air ahead of the big balloon show next week."

"That's good news," I said, because, at the time, I thought it was.

Brenda said, "I just know this is going to be the experience of my lifetime."

She was definitely right about that.

I handed Balloon Dave the wad of notes to pay for the flight. Luckily, I had more than enough to pay for Brenda too.

"Never had a kid book a flight before," he commented. "You said you had a guardian who would sign off on the paperwork?"

I pointed at Grandpa Frank. "Yeah – him. He's my Grandpa Frank. I'm looking after him." I liked how it sounded when I said that, and maybe I said it a bit proud-like, because Grandpa Frank looked over at me and caught my eye.

Balloon Dave shook Grandpa's hand. "Extraordinary

grandson you've got there."

When he said, "Yes, I know," I was properly shocked.

"You think I'm extraordinary?"

Grandpa Frank pulled at the knot of his tie like it had suddenly become too tight for his neck. "I certainly wouldn't describe you as ordinary, but don't be getting carried away and making a show of yourself."

That was easier said than done, but I managed to keep a lid on my delight.

Grandpa Frank signed off all the paperwork for me. He did this thing where he pretended to forget my name, which was daft because it's the same as his (except my middle name is John), and we all laughed. Then the oldies had to sign some waiver, which took a bit of time because there was a section where they had to list all their medications. Between them, Grandpa and Brenda could have opened up their own branch of Boots with all the drugs they were on.

"What do you take all that lot for?" I asked him.

He said, "Never you mind. But you don't keep a body in as excellent shape as mine without a bit of help."

I looked at his tummy and considered telling him

that he wasn't getting the right kind of help, but thought better of it.

Balloon Dave was very proud when he told us that he had the **biggest balloon basket in the county** – which was lucky because it could fit Brenda's wheelchair in no problem. He twiddled with some knobs on this massive gas-tank thing and said, "Are you ready for the experience of a lifetime?" He sounded just like Uncle Vinny when he's running the waltzers and says, "Scream if you want to go faster!"

As the experience of a lifetime was exactly what I was ready for, I said, "**YES!** I *am* ready for the experience of a lifetime."

Brenda whooped and Grandpa made a grumbly noise, which I chose to take as a positive grumbly noise rather than a negative grumbly noise.

All in all, things were going very well.

It only occurred to me when Dave had closed the door that hot-air ballooning essentially involves being thousands of metres in the air with only wicker under your feet. I grabbed hold of the side of the basket and thought about wicker for a moment. It wasn't the strongest of materials. I'm pretty sure the little pig's house made of wicker was easily blown down by the wolf. Wicker wouldn't be my first choice of flooring if I was designing a basket for a hot-air balloon. I'd probably choose that material aeroplanes are made out of.

Grandpa Frank must have noticed something was up, because he said, "You alright, Frank? You've gone a bit white."

"I'm fine," I said, even though I was having some substantially-sized misgivings. Wasn't there some wicker man who was set on fire? Why would anyone think a basket of wicker hanging under a great big flamethrower was a good idea?

"You sure you're okay?" Brenda studied me, her lips puckered like she was a gorilla sucking on a gobstopper. She made me think of all the monkeys I should have bought instead of spending my money on old people and wickery floating deathtraps.

There was no way I was going to tell them the truth. For one thing, I wasn't sure they'd understand why I was suddenly regretting not purchasing primates. And

I wasn't going to lose face, so I said what my dad would've said: "I'm smashing, thank you." And I tried my best to ignore my gut feeling that something was going to go massively wrong.

If I'd known that it was going to be Brenda who was in trouble and not me, I might have relaxed a little more.

CHAPTER 14

Take notice of the weather report

My dad doesn't really like to talk about the time he ended up dangling by his ankles from the top storey of the Waysafe supermarket car park in Woking. He'd borrowed some money from people he shouldn't have – which is the reason we moved. I can't say I blame him for his relunctance to speak. Revisiting trauma is not always a good thing, according to the bald doctor on one of Mum's favourite daytime TV chat shows. However, one thing Dad did say about the whole episode was that when you're a long way up and everything is a long way down, you're provided with a unique opportunity to gain a different perspective on things.

And by "things", I think Dad meant life.

Because after the police saved him from a face full of pavement, and again after he'd done his community service, Dad promised that he would find a more honest way of living – that he'd be a better dad. He said he'd seen "the bigger picture" up there on that car-park roof – that life was for living and living well. I suppose though, for Dad, living well always meant having loads of cash.

As we looked down from our rainbow-coloured hot-air balloon, I wondered if Grandpa Frank was experiencing a similar revelation about living.

"Does it make you realize there's a point to everything, being up here, seeing the world from a different perspective?"

Grandpa Frank shrugged. "It's a bit breezier than I imagined."

Maybe I needed to dangle him over the side by his bootlaces to achieve a more profound reaction.

There was a little window cut into the side of the basket which Brenda could see through. She seemed much more impressed by it all than Grandpa. She kept saying, "Oh, would you look at it all. Isn't it wonderful?

Makes you glad to be alive."

Now that was the sort of reaction I was after from Grandpa Frank. "Does it make you glad to be alive too, Grandpa?"

"Makes me wish I'd put on a vest," he said and tied up the straps of his deerstalker.

I'd spent a grand on that balloon flight – more money than I'd ever clapped eyes on – with the hope of making Grandpa Frank enjoy life, but all he was concerned about was it being a bit draughty. Okay, well it might have been more than a *bit* draughty, but still, he could have been more enthusiastic.

Once I was convinced that my concerns about wicker were completely unfounded, I really got on board with hot-air ballooning. It's possible – despite everything that happened later – that it is still one of my favourite forms of transport. Obviously it can't beat a camel, but it's up there.

Having lived in the area his whole life, Grandpa turned out to be an excellent tour guide. He pointed out the church that he and Grandma Nora got married in, and the hospital where my dad was born. The Soap

& Suds laundrette where they lost his suit trousers in 1978 and lied about it. The pub where he got his first pint. The park where he taught my dad to ride a bike. All sorts of cool stuff.

Balloon Dave said he could employ him as a sight-seeing guide he was so good.

I was enjoying myself so much that I wanted to have a go at flying the balloon myself, so I said, "Dave?" – I didn't call him Balloon Dave to his face – "Can I have a go at turning the fire up really high?"

He didn't seem to like that idea because he said, "Absolutely not. It's against all health and safety regulations. No one but me touches the burner. You have to have years of training to even turn the lever which opens the valve. Do you know what would happen to me if anyone found out? I'd lose my licence, that's what."

I decided to do what Dad would do in this situation. "I'll give you two hundred quid."

"Done."

Turning up the flame under a hot-air balloon is quite an exhilarating experience, because it means you lift up and it makes your stomach do a weird wobbly thing, which was a sensation I quite enjoyed. I had to stop after a bit though, because Brenda said the same sensation was making her need a wee and I did not want to be hundreds of metres up in the air with an old lady with a bladder problem and no toilet.

After I had stopped messing about with the gas, the wind really started to pick up. A couple of big gusts caused us all to stumble – or roll in Brenda's case – to one side of the basket. I'll admit it, I was getting a bit worried and started questioning the reliability of wicker all over again.

Grandpa Frank must have been getting a bit concerned too, because after Brenda had rolled into him for the third time, he said, "This alright, is it, Dave, this wind?"

I was expecting Balloon Dave to say that it was fine, but he chewed on his lip for a moment, checked his watch and then said, "Maybe it is time to land. I'll wait for an air current and see if I can turn us around and head back for the sports field."

At this point, landing seemed like an excellent option. My stomach had started to do the same clenching thing it did after I once accidentally ate a Munch Bunch yoghurt that I found at the back of the fridge, which turned out to be two years out of date.

The wind changed direction and turned the balloon back the way we'd come. I noticed the route we were taking back happened to take us over Mum's tennis club. I had a good look to see if I could see her – I thought she would be fairly easy to spot in her brightly coloured sports kit. I didn't see her, but I did see something else that caught my attention.

It was a car with a bonnet that was a different colour to the rest of the bodywork. Dad's new car. It stood out amongst all the silver Mercs and black Range Rovers. Mum wouldn't like Dad showing up there – in fact, I distinctly remember her telling him not to or she'd give him a close-up demonstration of her forehand smash.

I was about to point it out to Grandpa Frank but hesitated when someone got out of the front passenger seat. I knew who it was immediately. It was totally-tanned-Tony, Mum's tennis coach. I couldn't think for one second what Dad was doing talking to him.

But when a second man, who had his hair tied back

in a ponytail, climbed out of the back, I just knew that Dad was up to something dodgy again. Looking back now, maybe it was me who was seeing things more clearly from up in that balloon.

I didn't get a chance to dwell on it though, because of everything that happened with the balloon landing and poor old Brenda.

Prepare for the unexpected

While we were waiting for Brenda to have her check-up at the hospital, Balloon Dave told us he'd been up in that balloon over three thousand times and had never experienced anything like what happened to us. He said, "We're lucky to all still be alive, considering."

Grandpa Frank said, "I wouldn't use the word *lucky* to describe how I'm feeling right now."

I could see his point. Admittedly, it had been a fairly traumatic experience.

Even though I'd never been in a hot-air balloon before, I knew as soon as we started the descent that it wasn't exactly going to be a textbook landing. The first clue was when Balloon Dave told us to stay low with our heads in between our knees in the brace position. The wind was whipping up an absolute hooley by then. We were being bumped up and down and side to side. I was full up with panic, but Grandpa Frank seemed relatively unconcerned. I think maybe he was trying not to worry me.

Brenda put her hand on my knee and said, "All this rattling is going to set my dentures loose."

Grandpa Frank said, "It will all be over very quickly," and put his hand on my shoulder.

Which was nice, except that I thought he was referring to my life and couldn't stop myself from hollering, "I don't want to die!"

Even though we weren't exactly in a *ha-ha* funny situation, Grandpa Frank laughed at me.

I yelled, "How can you laugh at a time like this?"

He said, "You wally, I meant we'll be on the ground soon."

We weren't on the ground soon though. First, we smashed into the Soap & Suds laundrette's rooftop sign.

We walloped straight into it and the **OAP** of **SOAP** fell onto Brenda's lap.

Grandpa laughed even more and shouted, "That'll teach 'em to lie about my trousers." It's amazing, really, how some people can hold onto a grudge for so long.

Balloon Dave, however, was not laughing. He was pretty grim-faced, to be honest. He worked quickly, reinflating the balloon and then letting it down a little bit, until he had used the wind to manoeuvre us around the remains of the laundrette sign, away from the worried-looking people below us and into clear airspace.

I think this must have been the point at which one of the cables that was attached to the balloon somehow came loose and lashed itself around Brenda's wheelchair. But in all the excitement of a possible crash-landing and imminent death, nobody noticed.

Balloon Dave continued to work valiantly to try and keep the balloon under his control, but the wind was just too strong. He tried his best to avoid the trees that lined the back of the allotments, but they were the tall skinny type and they were swaying violently. We got a second big bump when we flew into their branches and I thought we were going to get stuck, but another giant gust of wind blew us off in another direction.

"We won't make the playing fields!" Balloon Dave shouted. "We'll have to make an emergency landing in Manor House Gardens."

At that point I wasn't too bothered where we landed,

as long as we landed. And in one piece.

Balloon Dave shouted, "Everybody get down and stay low while I try and land this thing."

From the wicker floor, it was quite apparent to me that the county's biggest balloon basket was proving too difficult for Balloon Dave to captain on his own in freakily high winds. Luckily Grandpa must have realized this too, because he tucked his tie down his T-shirt, jumped up and grabbed hold of Balloon Dave so he didn't fall overbasket. It made me quite proud, watching him try to save us.

We began to drop lower and lower, all the time swinging like a rainbow-coloured pendulum in the sky. There weren't many people in the park, probably on account of it being so windy. This was definitely a good thing, because it meant we were less likely to ruin somebody's day by landing a hot-air balloon on their head.

"Almost there, easy does it!" Balloon Dave said as he navigated us down. His face was still sweating but he didn't look quite as alarmed as he had done previously. "I think we're going to make it."

Grandpa Frank widened his stance. "Brace yourselves for a slight bump."

I braced myself for a slight bump...but what I got was a gigantic one. It felt like my bum bone was going to shoot up through my skull. I think Brenda's wheelchair was even airborne for a couple of seconds.

Balloon Dave pulled a rope to let the last of the air out of the balloon and it dramatically flopped down to one side. Grandpa slumped down on the basket floor next to me and Brenda.

Balloon Dave wiped his face with his big hands and said, "Thank you for flying with Dave's Fabulous Flights. I hope you have had a pleasant journey with us today." Then, a bit like his balloon, he sort of deflated from the bottom up and ended in a crumpled heap on the floor with the rest of us.

Nobody spoke for a while, but eventually we were able to crawl out onto solid ground. Balloon Dave wheeled out Brenda and set her on the grass next to me and Grandpa Frank. I wanted to take a photo of them in front of the hot-air balloon to document us surviving the first item on **Grandpa Frank's Bucket List**.

I gave Grandpa Frank the **OAP** sign to hold, pointed my phone at them and said, "Everybody smile. That means you too, Grandpa Frank."

Grandpa managed a thin-lipped smile of sorts and Balloon Dave...well, he still looked pretty traumatized if I'm honest. But Brenda smiled and put her thumbs up, because she didn't know what was about to happen next.

As soon as the words, "Everybody say **Old-Age Pensioners**!" had left my mouth, an almighty gust of wind blew across the park. Somehow, this inflated the balloon with enough air to propel it across the field – which wouldn't have been a massive problem, had Brenda's wheelchair not been attached to it by a stray balloon cable.

She hurtled over the grass at quite some speed, bouncing up and down in her wheelchair and shouting out some pretty choice words.

I don't think any of us knew what to do – it was just so unexpected – so we stood there and watched as the balloon and Brenda picked up more and more speed.

"Someone should do something," I said, with little

hope of anyone actually doing anything.

Grandpa nodded and said almost as unconvincingly, "Someone really should."

But we all carried on standing there, doing nothing, as she sped across the grass and straight into the duck pond. Which I suppose, all things considered, was the softest place for her to land.

CHAPTER 16

You're either a floater
or a sinker

When I had swimming lessons in Year Four, my swimming teacher said that people are either floaters or sinkers. Fortunately for Brenda, she was one of life's floaters, so whilst her wheelchair ended up at the bottom of the pond in Manor House Gardens with all the shopping trolleys, Brenda did not. She bobbed about on the water amongst a flock of these big old duck things, which Grandpa Frank told me were Canadian geese. Imagine that – geese all the way from Canada! I wasn't so worried about Brenda drowning then, more about her being pecked to death, but the geese weren't in the least bit interested in savaging her.

Which was a relief.

Anyway, Brenda was given a clean bill of health at the hospital. (Apart from her not being able to walk that well or see that well or hear that well, but she was like that before she went in the water.)

When we got back to Autumnal Leaves – Brenda in an ambulance and me and Grandpa in the minibus – I got the impression that Stephen was incredibly hurt and disappointed with us both, because he said, "I am incredibly hurt and disappointed with you both."

After some of the care staff had taken Brenda to her room, Stephen gave us a right dressing-down in the lounge in front of everybody. Grandpa and I both looked at the carpet to show we were suitably sorry, but he gave me a little smile and a wink when Stephen wasn't watching.

"Breaking out on foot is one thing, but to commandeer the minibus is quite another. Not only was it illegal, it was incredibly dangerous." Stephen's face got very red when he said that.

Grandpa and I both said, "Sorry, Stephen."

"And not only did you disappear without telling

anyone and steal the minibus, you took a resident hostage. Poor Brenda was waiting for a driver to take her to her acupuncture appointment and the next thing she knows she's on a hot-air balloon!" He was pacing around the room now. He'd got himself in quite a state, considering everything had turned out fine in the end.

"Maybe you do need to think about an electric perimeter fence after all. That would have slowed us down," I said.

Stephen stopped pacing to eyeball me.

"And, to be fair, Brenda was quite up for coming along."

He eyeballed me even harder. "And was she up for an impromptu swimming lesson? I don't think so! Brenda's eighty-seven years old, for goodness' sake. Imagine the stress of being dragged around a field by a hot-air balloon and then going for a quick dip in the pond with some Canada geese at that age."

It wasn't the right moment and it wasn't the right thing to do, but I couldn't help it – I started laughing. Then I heard a snort and I realized that Grandpa Frank was sniggering too.

Stephen threw his arms in the air and said, "I cannot believe you two! I'm sorry, Mr Davenport, but you leave me no choice – you've lost your TV privileges for two weeks." Then he marched out of the room in a bit of a strop.

I said, "Don't worry, Grandpa Frank, I'll buy you your own TV. I've got heaps of cash."

"So you keep saying." Then he said, "Anyway, I have a feeling that, what with this **Bucket List** of yours, I'm going to be a bit too busy to watch TV."

"You still want to carry on? After everything that happened today?"

Grandpa Frank cleared his throat and his voice got a little stiffer. "No choice, have I? Not if I want my villa in Spain."

"I suppose not." I'd kind of been hoping he wanted to do the list just to hang out with me. But then I remembered my reward. I suppose we both had our own reasons.

CHAPTER 17

Life's about compromises, like getting a dog instead of a monkey

That evening, Dad was out again, which made me wonder what he was up to. I kept thinking about the guy with the ponytail and why Dad had been talking to him in his car.

Rather than inflicting her cooking on me, Mum ordered a stuffed-crust pepperoni pizza, which she let me eat in front of the TV. I should have realized she was up to something too, because of the white-fluffy-rug no-food rule, but I was too busy eating and watching a very funny programme called **TV's Biggest Bloopers**.

I wasn't happy when she went and paused it.

"Hey, why did you stop it? I wanted to see what happened with the banana skin and that donkey."

She had a very stern face on, despite the programme being hilarious. "How are you doing, Frank?"

"I was fine until you stopped the show." I nodded at the remote for her to turn it on again, but she only went and turned the TV off completely. I threw a piece of pizza crust down on my plate to show her I wasn't happy.

"I want to talk about this thing with your grandpa."

"But now I'm never going to know what happened to that donkey!"

"Frank, would you be serious for a while?"

That's when I realized what was going on. Serious meant only one thing. She was angling to talk about the money.

"I know you've been to see your grandfather. What do you do with him all day? It can't be much fun hanging out with an old man."

"It's more fun than traipsing around with Dad or hanging out with you at the tennis club – I wish you'd never won that membership. Besides, it's not like I've got mates queuing up at the door to see me." I said that last bit quietly, so I don't think she heard.

She did this big sigh and said rather wearily, "Don't start that again, Frank," which I thought was cheeky, because she was the one who had started the whole conversation. If she'd let me find out about the donkey, I wouldn't be complaining about the tennis club.

"Tell me then, what do you do with your grandpa that is so fun?"

"Today, we went on a hot-air balloon flight and it was so windy we almost crashed. Well, we *did* crash, right into the Soap & Suds laundrette. But we survived, and Grandpa Frank helped land the balloon. He was pretty awesome, actually. Then Brenda ended up in the pond, but she floated, so it was all okay."

Mum blinked at me twice and then said, "Frank, what are you talking about?"

"I'm just telling you what I did with Grandpa Frank today."

Mum eyeballed me for a moment, picked up her plate and said, "There are things happening, Frank. Serious things. I'll speak to you when you're going to be sensible." And then she left the room. I could hear her banging about in the kitchen, muttering angrily to herself. I probably should have been wondering about what the serious things were, but I didn't actually want to know and, besides, I had the next activity on the **Bucket List** to organize.

I scarpered upstairs before she came back wanting to talk some more. I closed my bedroom door after sticking a note on the outside that said *KEEP OUT*. Then I pulled the **Bucket List** from my back pocket and checked through it to see which activity we should tackle next. Nothing too adventurous after the near-death ballooning incident, I thought.

It quickly became obvious to me which one I should choose. Learning to train a monkey definitely wouldn't be life-threatening, but it would be very enjoyable. However, after a bit of internet research and a phone call to the RSPCA for confirmation, I discovered monkey training is frowned upon. It's not considered an animal-friendly activity. It seemed like my monkey dream just wasn't meant to be. Sue from the RSPCA saved me from the crushing disappointment when she said, "If you want to learn to train something, you might want to start with a dog."

Grandpa Frank was bound to like dogs. Everybody likes dogs.

I said, "Thank you, Sue. That is an excellent idea," and set about sourcing a dog.

It took me a little while to figure something out; turns out it's easier to end up in charge of a grandpa than a canine. You have to be sixteen to buy one and there was no way that I'd pass for that old. And there's all sorts of checks to make sure that you'd be a good doggy owner.

It started to look like my dog quest was going the way of my monkey one but then I remembered the place where Mum has her hair done – Dogs and Do's.

It's a dog rescue and rehoming centre as well as a dog-groomer and hairdresser.

I told them about **Grandpa Frank's Great Big Bucket List** and Janice, the owner, said she had a wonderful dog we could borrow as it was such a good cause.

Once that was sorted, because I was feeling a bit

guilty about Brenda being stuck with a hospital wheelchair, I ordered her a brand-new top-of-the-range one in pink, gold and black leopard-print with fluffy armrests and lights on the spokes.

While I was at it, I also bought a few other things to turn the Autumnal Leaves games room into a room that would live up to its name.

I went to bed feeling pretty pleased with myself. I had done some properly good caring. I drifted off to sleep thinking about how I was doing brilliantly at carrying out my dead step-grandmother Nora's last request and wondering just how big my reward would eventually be.

CHAPTER 18

Everyone is a dog person really

I arrived at Autumnal Leaves early the next morning. Grandpa was in the lounge, scribbling angrily in a crossword book. I was excited to tell him about the next activity.

"A dog? You've got me a dog?" Grandpa Frank put his crossword book down on the coffee table.

I plonked myself onto a footstool. "Sort of. You're not allowed to keep it here. Stephen said no pets as, what with some of the residents' allergies, a dog could be lethal, so I decided to rent one for you. Besides, there's lots of rules and while you are over sixteen, I'm not sure you are responsible enough yet."

"What do you mean, you've *rented* me a dog?"

"Well, borrowed one, really."

"You've lost me."

I didn't think it was a difficult concept to understand, but Grandpa Frank seemed to be struggling with it. I wasn't going to explain the meaning of borrowing to him, so I pulled out my phone and opened the web page to read to him. "Dogs have been proven to offer a sense of well-being, companionship and even a reason for living. Sounds good, hey?"

He raised one of his bushy eyebrows. "Is that so?"

"Yup, it is, says so right here. I've always wanted a dog, but Mum doesn't want the hair in the house and Dad says they cost too much to keep."

"So why did you think I'd want one?"

"Because dogs are brilliant. And I thought it would be good for you. Dicky is going to give you a new lease of life. Maybe even make you happy."

"Dicky?"

"He's a Newfoundland. Like the dog out of *Peter Pan*."

"Aren't Newfoundlands enormous?"

"I thought if I was going to rent a dog for you, I may as well try and get as much mutt for my money as possible. And Dicky is a whole lot of dog."

Grandpa Frank shook his head and then said something which was a bit odd. He said, "Nora's not going to like it, son. And who's going to look after it when I'm at work?"

On reflection, I could have been a bit more tactful instead of blurting out, "Nora's dead, Grandpa, and you're way too old to have a job. You haven't had a job for years."

For a moment, he didn't look like himself. At the time I couldn't work out what the expression on his face was. But I know now. It was fear.

A good few seconds passed while he sat there, looking strange. I thought maybe I'd broken him again. I was about to wave my hands in front of his face and say, "Cuckoo! Anybody home?" to see if I could snap him out of it, but he suddenly seemed to remember where he was.

"A dog, you say?"

"Yeah, a dog. You alright, Grandpa? I thought I'd

153

lost you there for a minute."

"I'm fine. I'm simply trying to process the fact that you have rented me a humungous dog." He didn't sound fine, he sounded a bit shaky, but I didn't say any more about it. I just carried on like everything was normal, because that's what you do, isn't it?

"I know he's big but he's dead friendly, apparently. He should be easy enough to handle when you show him."

"What do you mean, *show* him?"

"You know, when you take him to a dog show and trot him around the ring and then get awarded a rosette for all the showing and trotting. **Competing in a dog show** is now one of the items on your **Bucket List**, so you have to do it."

"Frank, I have never, nor will I ever *trot*."

"You won't have to trot." He would, but he could find that out later.

"And I'm not really a dog person."

That was a ridiculous thing to say. There are only two types of people in the world: those who are dog people, and those who are but just don't know it yet.

"Would you prefer to stay here and paint a picture of a fruit bowl with the others?"

By the way he scrunched up his big old-guy nose, I could tell that thought didn't fill him with much glee. He glanced over to the table where Stephen was arranging a sad-looking banana, a pineapple and a shrivelled-up orange in a dish.

"Way I see it is this, Grandpa Frank – you can either stay here and do the same thing you've done every day for the past gazillion years, or you can come with me and do something new and take Dicky out for a stroll."

"Fine. If only to shut you up."

"You won't regret it!"

"You said that about the hot-air ballooning."

Dicky lived with Janice and Paul Gibson and around twenty other dogs just under a half-hour walk away at Dogs and Do's. This meant that we could walk there, avoiding the need to hijack any unroadworthy minibuses. When I'd spoken to Janice on the phone, she had told me Dicky was just over twelve. If I could do my seven times table, I'd be able to tell you exactly how old he was in human years, but I'll hazard a guess that he was around eighty. Which wasn't that dissimilar to Grandpa Frank, come to think of it. Janice also told me Dicky had been at Dogs and Do's for most of his life – they'd never managed to rehome him. When his first owners realized how big a dog he actually was, they decided they couldn't look after him any more. Which meant he'd been abandoned by his family. I suppose that was a bit like Grandpa Frank too, alone in his nursing home – at least until I came along with my **Bucket List** idea.

Janice and Paul described Dogs and Do's as a tri-purpose business, which is basically a fancy way of saying they run a dog-rescue centre, a dog-grooming parlour and a hairdresser all under one roof. Janice is in charge of the grooming and the hairdressing. She says they require a very similar skill set, which is apparent when you look at some of the hairdos her human customers come out with. Mum goes there, so I know what I'm talking about.

We met Paul and Dicky in the reception area of the

rescue centre. I'd seen a photo of Dicky but even that hadn't prepared me for how humungous he actually was – I'm talking the size of a small horse. Grandpa could have ridden him if he had wanted to. Which he didn't. I did ask.

When Grandpa clapped eyes on Dicky for the first time he said, "Well, slap me sideways, what in the name of sweet poochery is that supposed to be?"

It was hard not to say, "A dog," without sounding too patronizing.

Grandpa Frank pointed at Dicky. "That there is not a dog. That's a beast."

I quickly covered Dicky's big furry ears with my hands. "Grandpa Frank, you can't go saying that! You'll hurt his feelings."

Paul looked at Grandpa Frank, then flicked his long, straggly hair over his shoulder and said, in a voice which was so slow it almost made me feel a bit sleepy, "Dicky is one of our more sensitive residents."

Grandpa Frank spluttered, "The dog doesn't understand what we're saying!"

Which I didn't think was a very nice thing to say

when you're meeting your new pet for the first time, even if we were only borrowing him. Dicky obviously agreed with me, because he tilted his enormous head and did this little whimper.

Paul stroked Dicky's big flappy ears, then said to Grandpa Frank, "You'll have to apologize, or he may suffer irreparable psychological damage."

I couldn't believe it when Grandpa Frank laughed. Who finds a psychologically damaged dog funny? I said, "Grandpa, you need to apologize!" and I gave him a very hard stare so he knew I was serious.

Grandpa Frank looked a bit uncomfortable, but he still didn't say sorry. He said, "Oh, for goodness' sake. I'm not apologizing to a dog."

I glared even harder, Paul shook his head and Dicky did another sad little whine.

Grandpa Frank looked at each of us in turn. He was outnumbered and in the wrong, so I didn't see what choice he had.

"Grandpa Frank, just say you're sorry. It isn't hard."

After an almighty huff, he said, "I can't believe I'm doing this but, Dicky, I'm sorry."

I gave Grandpa Frank a triumphant nod and Dicky gave him a big fat lick on his hand, which he then made a big show of wiping off. I think we all knew, though, that some excellent old-grouchy-man and massive-rental-dog bonding had occurred.

CHAPTER 19

Old people can learn new tricks

Paul handed Dicky's lead to Grandpa Frank and said, "So the plan for today is as follows. Frank, you and Dicky are going around to the grooming parlour where Janice will meet you. She'll show you how to make Dicky look sensational for the dog show this afternoon."

"Dog show? This afternoon? But I don't know how to show a dog."

Paul put his hand on Grandpa Frank's shoulder. "Don't worry, dude, I know you and Dicky have only just met, but it's a beginners' show – we'll teach you what to do. It's basically just a bit of leading and trotting. Nothing to stress about."

Grandpa Frank glared at me. "I do not trot."

Paul smiled slowly. "Chill, **Grandpappy D**. I'm sure we'll find something you're cool with."

Even though neither of us had met her before, Janice was absolutely delighted to see us. She was wearing a T-shirt which said **Short Bark 'n' Sides** and had a lot of orangey-blonde hair which reminded me a bit of a spaniel's ears. She bounced up and hugged me and Grandpa Frank in turn. Grandpa Frank did not do a good job of hiding the fact he was not a natural hugger, and pulled the same face as when Dicky licked him.

"I have to say, when your grandson told me about the Bucket List, I thought *what a brilliant idea*. You're going to just love working with Dicky, he really is the most placid of dogs. So gentle, so kind, never causes us any trouble."

Thinking about it now, it's hard to believe those words came out of her mouth. But I suppose she wasn't to know what would happen.

She linked her arm through Grandpa Frank's and, before he could complain, she swept him out through a door and along a corridor which was covered in

Dalmatian-print wallpaper. Grandpa Frank kept hold of Dicky's lead and the big dog padded along obediently beside him. Which I realize now was all a clever scam to lull everyone into a false sense of security.

I followed along behind until we reached a door with a sign that said, **Welcome, Wagstar!** Janice flipped it over and the other side said, **Pooch Pampering in Progress – Please Don't Disturb.**

She did this high-pitched squeal, clapped her hands together and said, "Are you ready, gorgeous boy?"

Grandpa Frank stifled a little smile and said, "Well, er, yes. I suppose I am."

Janice said, "Oh, I meant Dicky! But yes, you can be gorgeous too!"

Grandpa Frank went bright red and stammered something about knowing that's what she meant all along.

Janice unlinked her arm and opened the door. "Now, **Grandpa Gorgeous**—"

"There's really no need for that." He still looked mortified.

She walked over to a huge contraption in the middle

of the room and said, "This here is an extra-large hydraulic dog-grooming table. When I have lowered it, I'd like you to give Dicky the order to climb on."

Grandpa didn't look certain. "How do I do that?"

Janice smiled. "Just say, 'Climb on, Dicky!'"

She pressed a button and the table lowered. Grandpa looked at me and I gave him an encouraging nod. He said, a little hesitantly, "Climb on, Dicky."

I think we were all a bit surprised when Dicky padded onto the table.

"Well done, Mr Davenport. You're a natural handler. He must like you."

Grandpa Frank smiled this great big smile. "Well, I'll be blown. What a clever dog. Didn't I say he was a clever dog?"

Because I was so delighted that Grandpa had done it, I didn't think it was worth pointing out that less than half an hour earlier he'd called Dicky a beast who didn't understand anything.

I guess it just goes to show how quickly you can change your opinion about things.

Throughout the two-hour grooming session,

Grandpa did exactly as he was told and so did Dicky. In fact, Janice said they both "behaved beautifully" and if they carried on like that then they had a good chance of maybe even winning the dog show. I think the idea of winning appealed to Grandpa Frank, because he started paying really close attention to everything Janice said. Shame, really, that Dicky had other ideas.

Eventually, after a lot of brushing and combing and trimming, Janice stood back and held Grandpa's hand and said, in quite a dramatic manner, "Our work here is done."

Now, not to diss Janice's work because I know she was runner-up in the Kent County Dog-Grooming Championships in 2011, but apart from a big blue bow, I struggled to see much difference in how Dicky looked after the grooming session compared to before. Grandpa Frank, however, thought Dicky looked "Truly magnificent". Those were his exact words. He was looking at Dicky with soppy, proud eyes. And even though Dicky might not have changed much, I suppose something must have changed in Grandpa.

I didn't know what it was at the time. Now, I think he

must have got the fuzzy warm feeling you get from looking after somebody else.

I caught myself in the mirror and realized I was looking at Grandpa just like that too.

CHAPTER 20

Take a ride in a dogmobile, you won't regret it

I was delighted that we got to travel to the dog show in the Dogs and Do's van, because Paul and Janice had decked it out to look like an enormous Labrador. There was a massive dog head on the roof with this big pink tongue, and the bodywork was covered in fur. When you pressed the horn it didn't honk, it barked. It's up there with my favourite ways to travel. Really, **travelling in a dogmobile** deserves its own place on a **Bucket List**.

The dog show was the big finale of a fête being held in Manor House Gardens – the place with the pond and the geese all the way from Canada. Considering the disaster we'd had there only the day before, the location could have been a sign that we should worry. We didn't though. All I could say was, "Look, you can still see Brenda's tyre tracks in the grass," and Grandpa was far too busy practising the commands Paul and Janice had gone through with him. At this point, Dicky was doing exactly as he was told, and Grandpa Frank said he was supremely confident of the win.

"It's all in your attitude," he told me while Paul and Janice went to register for the show. "Us Davenports are born winners, Frank. You hear what I'm saying?"

"That's what Dad thinks too. In fact, he said exactly those words about us being winners."

"He did, did he?" Grandpa looked at me out the side of his eye and sat down on a park bench. Dicky sat himself down at his feet, looking massive and fluffy and obedient and giving away no clues whatsoever as to what he was plotting.

"Yup, right before he won a monkey."

"Your father won a what?"

I plonked myself down on the bench next to him. "Five hundred quid."

"Ah, I see."

"Down the bookies."

"Your father needs to learn to stay out of that place."

"That's what Mum says. She reckons Dad would bet on the colour of the Queen's knickers if he could."

Grandpa Frank shook his head and said to Dicky, "What do you do about that, hey, big fella?"

Because Dicky didn't answer, I said, "Maybe you should have a word with Dad. Not about the Queen's knickers, about the gambling."

"It's been years since we spoke. Don't care to think about how many. Besides, he's never listened to anything I've had to say – he's not going to start now. I don't want to discuss it."

"That's not a very winning attitude. Thought you were a Davenport. He's your son, you should look out for him."

I must have hit a sore spot because Grandpa Frank snapped at me, "Don't get involved in things you know nothing about." He stood up like he was about to leave and said, "Things are complicated between me and your dad. You wouldn't understand, you're only a kid."

Then he looked at Dicky and said, "Come on, boy, we're off," like he thought Dicky was on his side. Dicky definitely wouldn't have been on his side.

I couldn't quite believe he'd said I was *only* a kid. How was I only a kid? "I am not ONLY a kid," I said. "I'm your carer, old man!"

He can't have liked that because he shouted over his shoulder, "I don't know what it is you think you're doing, but I wouldn't say almost killing me with a hot-air balloon is caring."

"What do you mean, *with* a hot-air balloon?" He made it out like I'd hit him round the back of the head with it.

He hollered back, "The sooner I get through this ridiculous list of yours and get my villa in Spain, the better." He disappeared off into a crowd of people who were watching some morris dancers waving hankies and banging sticks. He and Dicky stomped right through the middle like they owned the place.

That annoyed me so much I kicked a stone into the pond and then I felt bad because I startled the geese. Grandpa Frank was wrong about me not being a proper carer. How could he say that when I'd gone to the trouble of doing a **Bucket List**? I was doing excellent caring. Reward-winning caring.

He was right about one thing though – I didn't understand what the problem was between him and my dad. I had a strong feeling that it might be something to do with their stubbornness though. And that's when it struck me. I took out the folded piece of paper from my back pocket, asked a passer-by for a pen and wrote a final entry onto my **Bucket List**, underlining it twice to show I really meant it.

Make my dad and Grandpa Frank
be friends again.

CHAPTER 21

Remember things can go wrong at any point

To deal with the angry feelings I was having towards Grandpa Frank, I went to the ice-cream van and bought myself a ninety-nine and paid an extra few quid to have five flakes, sprinkles and all the sauces. Soon, I wasn't feeling cross any more. I was feeling sick. Maybe getting everything you want all at once isn't all it's made out to be.

Because I wasn't going to be the one to go and apologize, I sauntered around the stalls. I had a go on the tombola and the lucky dip and bought myself some candyfloss – which wasn't my cleverest idea, because I felt even sicker after eating it. I was considering whether a bottle of blue raspberry pop would help my stomach situation or make it worse, when the tannoy did this really loud screech and everyone in the park groaned and covered their ears.

A posh-sounding woman said, "The Dog Showing competition shall commence in the fenced-off area in the centre of the park in ten minutes. Would all competitors make their way there now, please? Late entrants will be disqualified."

I could see Janice and Paul were already over there, but Grandpa Frank and Dicky weren't. I scanned the park to see where they'd got to. It wasn't too difficult to spot them, on account of Dicky being the size of a gorilla. They were back at the bench we'd been at before.

Grandpa Frank didn't look like he was making any effort to get to the dog ring. I stomped over. "What are you doing? You need to get to the show ring."

He looked at me and said, in a very small voice, "I can't remember where I am."

I pulled a face. "Is the pressure of showing Dicky getting to you or something?" because I honestly

172

thought that was what was up with him. I probably should have thought a little more.

He looked at Dicky like he'd only just noticed there was a dog the size of a lion next to him.

I grabbed his hand and pulled him to his feet. "Grandpa, come on, you're going to miss it."

He pulled his arm from mine. "Grandpa?"

"You want me to call you something else?"

He did this double take and looked from me to Dicky then over at the dog ring. It felt like an absolute age passed before his eyes became less cloudy and he said, "Yes, right, the dog show."

I said, "Are you okay?" because I was beginning to suspect he might not be. Maybe the stress of competing was getting to him. Or maybe it was something else, although I don't think I was ready to admit that then.

He tucked his top into his trousers and said, in a bit of a defensive tone, "I'm fine. Quit hassling me."

We made it to the arena with seconds to spare. The other competitors were all lined up. There was a really snooty-looking King Charles spaniel, a cockapoo who came across as a bit needy, a very teeny dog that looked

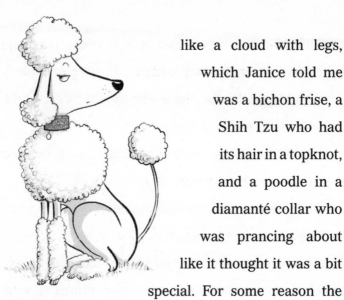

like a cloud with legs, which Janice told me was a bichon frise, a Shih Tzu who had its hair in a topknot, and a poodle in a diamanté collar who was prancing about like it thought it was a bit special. For some reason the poodle reminded me of Mum. To be honest, I didn't think any of them looked like any real competition for Dicky.

Janice, however, had got herself into a bit of a flap. She was glaring at the poodle, saying, "I cannot believe they've entered Patricia. She's not a beginner-level dog. She was on the front of *Pretty Pooches* magazine last month, for puppies' sake!"

Paul was trying to calm Janice down by saying, "It's just a bit of fun, love," but Janice wasn't having any of it.

Grandpa Frank, however, having regained his composure, seemed very calm about the whole situation. He bent down and ruffled Dicky's fur and said – very wrongly, as it turned out – "That trophy's coming home with us. Not a dog here who's a match for you, hey, Dicky?"

But Dicky wasn't looking at Grandpa. Dicky was looking at Patricia the poodle.

There was quite a crowd gathered around the arena and even I was beginning to get a bit nervous. Grandpa and Dicky were the second-to-last up, and as we watched the performances of the competitors that went before them, we began to think they might actually stand a chance. Colin the cockapoo had started off well but then refused to walk up the little see-saw and wouldn't move from in between his owner's legs. To be fair to **Barbara, the bichon frise**, she didn't have a bad run but, bless her, she took a fair few goes at the jumps, probably because she had such tiny little legs.

The Shih Tzu only got halfway round because she stopped for a wee on one of the fences, which apparently was a disqualification-worthy offence. **Lady, the King Charles spaniel**, completed the whole course perfectly, but no way was she prepared to do it at any kind of speed. She stalked around with her nose in the air, completely ignoring the requests of her owner to find another gear.

When the announcer said, "Next we have Dicky, a Newfoundland and our biggest dog competing today, with his owner, Mr Frank Davenport," all the ice cream and candyfloss in my stomach must have mixed together with my nerves, because I did a surprise sick-burp. It tasted alright, so I swallowed it back down.

The bouncy, smiley Janice we had met at the salon had disappeared under the stress of a competitive dog show. Bouncy Janice had been replaced by angry-shouty Janice. Paul was looking at her with these humungous, nervous eyes. She put both hands on Grandpa Frank's shoulders and shouted, "You've got this, Mr Davenport," like if he didn't, she wouldn't be happy about it.

Grandpa looked at Dicky and said, "No, *we've* got this," and off he trotted, into the ring.

Yes, *trotted*. It turns out Grandpa Frank will trot if he thinks there's a chance of a trophy.

Although it was a bit of a squeeze, Dicky managed to get through the long plastic tunnel. He also weaved in and out of the poles with no trouble. He totally nailed the see-saw – Janice threw Colin's owner a smug little smile at that point.

Then he jumped over the low fence, ran through another set of poles, over a couple more fences and across the finish line. A perfect run!

The announcer said, "How about a big cheer for a big dog! Well done, Dicky, and his owner, Mr Frank Davenport! That puts them in first place with only

Patricia the poodle to go!" All the people watching did as they were told and cheered, but I think they would have done it out of choice anyway.

He was out of breath, but Grandpa Frank looked thrilled. He bowed to the crowd with this big grin plastered across his face and his chest all puffed up. Dicky must have known things had gone well because he was jumping up and licking Grandpa and Grandpa was stroking his coat furiously. It was quite cute to see.

Unfortunately, Dicky's moment of victory was somewhat overshadowed by the events that happened next. Although, to be honest, Patricia the poodle should shoulder her part of the blame.

CHAPTER 22

Sometimes, it's hard to let go

You know when sometimes things go catastrophically wrong and, while you are watching them go catastrophically wrong, everything seems to go in slow motion? You can see everything unravelling in front of you, but you can't do anything about it? Well, that didn't happen at the dog show. It all happened so quickly that it took me quite a while afterwards to piece together exactly what went down.

We were all anxiously waiting to see whether Grandpa would cling onto first place, when Patricia sauntered past Dicky on her way to the ring. She stopped. She waggled her backside in his face and then SNIFFED his bum!

Well, I don't think Dicky liked that at all. While Patricia began her run around the ring, Dicky started pulling at his lead like he wanted to chase after her. He probably wanted to have a word with her about the whole uninvited bum-sniffing thing.

The thing is, when a massive dog like Dicky pulls on their lead, the person on the other end knows about it. And when that person is an elderly man like Grandpa Frank, only one thing is going to happen – they're going to get pulled over. And that's exactly what did happen.

Grandpa Frank didn't do what he should have done and let go of the lead. No, rather stubbornly, he held onto it. And Janice, Paul and I didn't do what we should have done and help, we just stood there, watching everything unfold.

Clearly, Dicky was a dog on a mission. He was going to have it out with Patricia, and no one was going to stop him. He pounded into the arena, paying no attention to the posh announcer woman, who was ordering him to, "Sit, bad dog! Sit!"

He charged through the plastic tunnel and Grandpa

Frank was dragged through after him. They both shot out the other side like a one-man-one-dog bobsleigh team.

Patricia caught sight of Dicky at this point. She knew he was after her, so, much to the dismay of her owner, she abandoned her run midway through and legged it. But Dicky wasn't going to let her go that easily. He went after her and, because Grandpa Frank was *still* holding on, Grandpa Frank went after her too.

The crowd parted as Patricia raced through with Dicky and Grandpa Frank in hot pursuit. She weaved around the group of morris dancers, who were having a tea break from all their hanky-waving. Dicky and Grandpa Frank didn't so much weave as crash through them and they all fell off their plastic chairs, ending up in a big heap of jingling bells on the grass.

At this point, I realized it might be a good idea to try and do something, so I gave chase. Patricia ducked under the lucky-dip table, followed by Dicky and Grandpa, who smashed straight into it, showering themselves in shredded paper and cheap plastic toys. But even that wasn't enough to slow them down.

Patricia headed off towards the far end of the park, where the field curved down to the pond. Dicky bounded across the grass and, even though he had an octogenarian hanging onto his lead, it didn't look like that was holding him back – in fact, he was gaining ground on the poodle.

At the time, I didn't know what Patricia's plan was, as she'd essentially cornered herself between Dicky and the water.

But now I think Patricia knew exactly what she was doing. She suddenly stopped completely still, right at the water's edge, and looked over her shoulder straight at Dicky. Dicky slammed on the brakes and managed to stop in time. Grandpa Frank, however, did not. He carried on going and somehow flipped over Dicky's head and went face first into the pond. Very close to Brenda's entry point, as it happened.

Grandpa splashed about for a bit, spluttering and spitting out water and angry comments. Then he stood up, stuck his sopping wet deerstalker back on his head and waded to the edge of the pond. I offered him a hand to try and pull him out, but he didn't seem to be in a hand-holding mood. He stomped off up the bank, yelling all sorts of things at me, like, "I wanted to be left on my own, but *no*, you wanted me to *do things*," and "'This will be fun', you said," and "'Have goals, not regrets', you said."

It's fair to say, at that exact moment, Grandpa probably wasn't living his best life.

Dicky and Patricia seemed to be living theirs though. It turned out Dicky didn't want to have a go at her for sniffing his bum, he just wanted to have a sniff of hers.

It was a quiet drive back to Autumnal Leaves. Even the barking horn couldn't raise a smile from Janice or Grandpa Frank. Dicky sat in the back, apparently unaware of the drama he had caused. He was obviously thinking about something else, because he kept doing these long sighs and he had this dopey grin on his face.

Even though I was a bit scared to ask, eventually I plucked up enough courage to say to Grandpa, "Why didn't you just let go of the lead?"

He said, "I don't know. I guess I thought I might lose Dicky."

I guess we all hold onto things we shouldn't a little too tightly. Sometimes it's giant dogs, other times it's grudges.

When we got back to Autumnal Leaves, Stephen came out onto the drive and was in the process of saying, "Wow, what a brilliant Labrador van," when Grandpa Frank climbed out of the passenger seat.

Stephen clapped his hands over his mouth, then said, "Mr Davenport, are you wet?"

Grandpa Frank didn't answer, just glared at him, so it was down to me to explain. "He fell in the pond at Manor House Gardens because Dicky was after a sniff of Patricia's bum."

Stephen's eyes bulged. "Who was sniffing whose bum?"

I was about to explain further, but then he held his hand up and said, "Actually, I don't want to know." He shook his head and said, "Would you look at the state of you, Mr Davenport! That's two of my residents in that pond in two days. What on earth were you doing?"

Grandpa Frank strode right by him, water dripping from the ear flaps of his deerstalker, and said, "**Living my best life**. *Apparently.*"

I shouted after him, "I'll see you on Friday, so I can sort out activity three. It'll be a good one, I promise!"

He didn't say anything, just threw his hands in the air, but I already knew he wasn't going to give up on the list. He was a Davenport, after all.

He'd make it all the way to the end. To the part where I'd surprise him and Dad and take them to see the Addicks play, and they'd both remember what was important and they'd make friends again. The part where Grandpa would stop Dad getting into trouble and Mum would stop needing to be so stressed.

The part where we could all be a proper family.

A happy family.

CHAPTER 23

Pay attention when paying for stuff on the internet

I didn't tell Mum about what Grandpa and I had been up to that day. She hadn't believed me about the hot-air ballooning, so I doubted she'd take me seriously about the dog show. Instead I let her think that I'd been at Autumnal Leaves, playing cards and watching TV. It just seemed easiest that way.

I was up in my bedroom organizing a **swimming-with-dolphins** experience for the coming Friday when Dad showed up, and if he hadn't have caused such drama, I might have paid more attention to what I was booking. As it was, when I heard the commotion going on outside, I just clicked the *pay now* button, then ran downstairs to see what was happening.

I opened the front door to see a car speeding off and my dad lying on the grass. It was obvious he wasn't in a good way because he had a black eye and he was bleeding from his nose. "Help me up, Frank," he said, "I'm not in a good way."

It wasn't the first time I'd seen Dad get himself into a scrape, but it still shocked me. I stood there gawping at him, doing nothing.

Mum appeared behind me and immediately started yelling at him, "What have you gone and done to yourself now?" like she thought that would help the situation. Then she said, "Get up and stop bleeding all over my front lawn. What must the neighbours be thinking?"

I helped Dad to his feet and brought him inside. I went to take him into the sitting room, but Mum put a stop to that by saying, "If he gets blood on my rug, I'll give him—"

She didn't reveal what she would give him, probably because she saw the look on my face. Instead she said, "Don't worry, Frank, everything is fine," although it

189

was fairly obvious that it wasn't.

I sat Dad down at the kitchen table and Mum got out the first-aid kit. She started wiping the blood off his face with an antiseptic wipe, which made him wince. When it was all cleaned up, she got a packet of frozen peas out and pressed them onto his eye.

And then she started crying. Which caught me by surprise, because she'd been doing such a good job of acting cross and not upset.

She stroked her hand over Dad's face and said, "Oh, Frank, what am I going to do with you?"

And he said, "I'm sorry, love. Really, I am. Please forgive me. I just don't know what to do. Things have been going so wrong and I can see everything unravelling in front of me, but I can't do anything to stop it."

Which was exactly how I had felt when Dicky had chased off with Grandpa. And probably how Grandpa felt when he didn't let go.

Because I didn't really know how I could help and because they'd both forgotten I was there, I went back up into my bedroom, put on my pyjamas and got into bed. I could hear snatches of conversation from downstairs.

Mum said something like, "Who did this to you, Frank?"

And Dad said, "I don't know, Tan."

But he did know. He just didn't want to say.

I didn't think I'd be able to sleep because I was too worried about Dad, but I must have drifted off at some point, because when I next looked at the clock it said 6.00 a.m., which is still the middle of the night in my book.

I tried to get back to sleep but I couldn't convince my body that it didn't need a wee. On the way back from the toilet, I spotted Dad coming out of the sitting room and heading to the front door.

I whispered down from the landing, "You alright now, Dad?"

He smiled at me. "I'm smashing, son. You okay?"

I shrugged. "Bit worried about you, I guess."

"Don't you be worrying about your old man, Frank. You know me. Always fine in the end."

"I want you to come and see Grandpa Frank." I don't

know why I said it then, at that moment, but the words just came out of me. Maybe it was because he looked like someone who needed a father.

Dad ran his hand through his hair. "I dunno, Frank. Too much stuff has happened that I can't forgive. You're too young, you wouldn't understand."

That annoyed me. Like being young means you can't understand things. From where I was sitting, it seemed like it was all the adults who had a problem with understanding. I tried to explain it to him in another way. "You're always asking Mum to forgive you. Why can't you forgive Grandpa?"

He said, "That's different," even though it wasn't. "He left me when I was just a kid. That man doesn't care about me."

"But I think he does. He just doesn't know how to show it. Maybe if you just—"

"People don't change, Frank."

I couldn't believe those words had come out of his mouth. Because of the frustration building up in my chest, my voice got a little bit squeaky when I said, "You're always telling Mum you'll change. And people *can* change, if you help them. Grandpa Frank didn't think he was a dog person and now he is."

Dad sighed. "What's that got to do with anything?"

I couldn't understand how he still wasn't getting it. "I just think you should forgive him, that's all. I've forgiven you."

"You've forgiven me? What do you mean by that?"

"I've forgiven you for the fact that you've never taken me to a footie game even though you keep saying you will. For the fact that you always mess up. That you're always up to something. That we have to keep moving every time one of your plans backfires. That you're the reason that I don't have any mates. That you care more about making money than you care about me."

Dad closed his eyes for a moment. Well, his right eye – the other one was already swollen shut from the bruising. When he opened it again, he said, "Whatever I've done, I've done it because I want the best for you and your mother. I want you to know that."

I said, "I know, Dad," even though I wasn't completely convinced. And then I said, "I've forgiven you because

I think that's what you have to do with family. People make mistakes. That's just what happens. And I think you moved near to him because some part of you wants to forgive him."

"I don't know about that, Frank."

"Don't you think you could forgive him, Dad? Please. He's old and he might kick the bucket soon and then you won't be able to forgive him because he'll be dead, and I think forgiving dead people probably isn't as effective as forgiving live ones."

Dad looked down at the floor and shook his head. "I'm sorry, son. It's just not a great time at the moment."

He opened the latch on the door and then he was gone, and I was left standing there, staring into the space he'd left, wondering why everything had to be so difficult. And why he spent so much time chasing after a better life in all the wrong places.

CHAPTER 24

Everyone likes a bucking bronco

When I arrived in a taxi at Autumnal Leaves on Friday, Brenda was outside to greet me in her new top-of-the-range wheels. She was "tickled pink" with them – her words, not mine. She did a little wheelie and said, "Well worth a dip in the pond for, Frank!" and then she zoomed off, the lights on her spokes flashing and hip-hop music blaring out of the speaker which Brenda must have had added onto the back.

Inside, Stephen ran out from behind the reception desk with a massive grin on his face. "You have to see this!"

He grabbed me by the elbow and practically dragged

me through to the games room. He flung open the doors and I gasped, then said, "Now *this* is what I call a games room!"

Down one end of the room, two little old women were having a game of tennis. Not real tennis, virtual tennis. They had these big VR goggles on and were waving their arms around aggressively.

Stephen pointed at one of them and said, "See Mary?"

"The one who looks a bit like a dried apricot with a blonde wig?"

"My goodness, so she does. Well, we all thought she had crippling arthritis."

Apricot Mary suddenly shouted, "Deuce! I'll take you yet, Dorothy!"

Stephen chuckled. "Appears that might not be the case." He then pointed at an old guy who was playing on the golf simulator, which was a bit of an impulse buy, to be honest. "And it turns out that Arnold used to play off scratch. Imagine that, a semi-pro golfer at Autumnal Leaves." Stephen shouted over to him, "How's it going, Arnold?"

Arnold waved his club at us. "Haven't picked up a club in years, but you know what? This old boy's still got it!"

Stephen stared at me with such kind, smiley eyes, I didn't know where to look. "It's amazing what you've done here. I spent an hour this morning on the light-up dance floor, battling against Esther. She's eighty-eight, Frank, eighty-eight! And I haven't even shown you the queue for the bucking bronco or the bungee run outside. You've given these old folk a new lease of life, you really have."

I was pretty pleased about that, but I was more keen to catch up with Grandpa Frank and tell him about the dolphins. "Have you seen my grandpa anywhere?"

Stephen checked his watch. "He should be back from his morning walk soon. He's gone to take that massive dog out the last few days. Gave us a bit of a scare yesterday when he couldn't remember the way back, but he was determined to go again today. That nice lady Janice said she'd make sure he gets home okay."

"He's been looking after Dicky? Really?"

I'd thought that, what with being dragged along on his face and then ending up in the pond, he might not want to see Dicky again. I'd pegged Grandpa as the type to hold a grudge. Maybe I was wrong about that.

Stephen said, "Every morning and every evening since you left on Tuesday!"

I waited outside the front of the building for Grandpa to get back. When I saw his deerstalker over the hedge, I ran to meet him.

"I'm so glad you and Dicky are still friends," I told him as we waved goodbye to Janice and Dicky.

"It wasn't his fault, and besides, I can understand somebody chasing after something they want, no matter the cost." He said that a bit wistfully and, although I wasn't sure, I had a feeling Grandpa was talking about something a bit deeper than Dicky trying to catch a whiff of Patricia's bottom.

When we were back in his room, I told Grandpa the good news about the **swimming-with-dolphins** experience I'd booked.

I did not get the enthusiastic response I was expecting. Instead he said, "I was hoping that the next thing on the **Bucket List** might not involve water."

"It's not my fault you don't know how to let go. All you had to do was drop the lead at any point between the arena and the pond."

"I don't want to talk about it."

"Good, neither do I. Let's talk about swimming with dolphins instead."

"Don't understand the appeal myself," he said, "swimming with giant fish."

"They're mammals not fish and don't tell me you don't want to swim with dolphins. Literally everybody wants to swim with dolphins!"

"Literally, they don't."

I was going to argue with him some more about that very wrong comment, but then a horn tooted outside – our taxi was waiting.

I said, "It's **Bucket List** time, Grandpa Frank. Grab yourself a towel, we're off to swim with dolphins."

Except we weren't. Well, not the kind of dolphins I had in mind anyway.

CHAPTER 25

There's more than one type of dolphin

The taxi pulled up outside the address I'd given and the first thing I said to the driver was, "Are you sure you've got this right?"

He said, "Satnav don't lie, kid."

"But it's a leisure centre. You don't get dolphins in a leisure centre."

The driver didn't seem bothered about that though, because he said, "I'm paid to get you from A to B, kid. I don't care whether there are dolphins or any other aquatic animals at B when I get there."

Grandpa Frank and I got out of the car and walked up the steps of Lewisham leisure centre. In my head, I was still thinking that maybe they'd specially transported some dolphins into the pool to swim with us.

I went up to the reception desk, where there was a man wearing a turquoise polo shirt and a badge saying **Be stronger than your excuses.**

"I'm Jamal," he said, "how can I help you today?"

"Hello, Jamal, we're both Frank," I said, "and we've booked to swim with the dolphins."

He did quite a twinkly smile. "First time?"

We both nodded.

Jamal said, "Those dolphins are something else," and I still thought he was talking about the friendly type you find in the ocean. He handed us a key to locker number thirteen – which should have been a sign luck wasn't on our side – and said, "Your swimsuits are in there. Get changed and the trainer will meet you poolside."

I remember thinking, *Trainer, now that sounds promising.*

Jamal buzzed us through the turnstile, and we headed to the changing rooms, still partly believing we were going to be swimming with dolphins in a leisure centre in Lewisham. I can't say my brain was operating at its brightest at that moment.

Grandpa Frank opened locker number thirteen and immediately said, "You've got another thing coming, lad, if you think you're going to see me in that get-up."

Hanging up were two, one-piece, knee-length swimsuits – one small, one large. Each had a picture of a pineapple on the front and both were covered in sequins.

I said, "I don't understand," because I didn't.

Grandpa Frank exhaled slowly through what was left of his teeth. "In the name of all things holy, why would we need to wear spangles to swim with dolphins?"

It was a puzzler. "Maybe the dolphins like sequins... and pineapples?"

Grandpa looked at me like I'd just turned into a tropical fruit myself.

"Look, I've paid good money for this." I didn't really know if I had because I'd paid zero attention when I'd booked it, what with Dad turning up like he did, but I was trying to be motivational. "I think we should get on and do it. What's it they say? You regret the things you don't do, not the things you do do?"

"I have two words for you. Dog and pond."

"Leave it out! You love Dicky now. And if you do it, you're one step closer to that villa in Spain."

He snatched up the bigger of the two swimming costumes. "Fine. I'm not too proud to wear a sparkly swimming costume."

He was too hairy to wear one though. Waaaaay too hairy. But once he had it on, I didn't see the point in telling him that. Instead I said, "It's lovely. Brings out the colour of your eyes."

He said, "I don't want another word out of you, sunshine."

So off we went through the horrible cold footbath onto the poolside, where we were greeted by **the Dolphins**.

A veterans' synchronized-swimming team for people of advanced years. Seven ladies wearing orange costumes and green swimming hats to make them look like human pineapples.

Not the aquatic mammals we had been expecting.

Grandpa just looked at me and said, "Frank, you complete and utter numpty."

There wasn't much I could say to that. Only a numpty would accidentally pay a joining fee to a senior-citizen synchro club instead of paying for a **swimming-with-dolphins** experience.

The trainer blew sharply on a silver whistle which was hanging around her neck and introduced herself as Ms Florence Kay. She had hair like lilac candyfloss, wrinkly skin like a sultana and was wearing an awful lot of make-up. In fact, all the women who made up **the Dolphins** were wearing an awful lot of make-up.

Florence turned to Grandpa Frank and said, "Mr Davenport, we're delighted you have come to join us for the morning. We shall be taking you through a few routines and, if we like you and you like us, we can talk about a place on the team. We need an eighth member for some of our new numbers." She didn't bother lowering her voice when she said, "Kathleen doesn't have a partner and if we don't get someone soon, frankly, she'll have to go."

A woman I guessed was Kathleen let out a little wail. Florence blew her whistle and said, "Keep it together, Kathleen. Synchro is not the sport for sobbing. You want to cry, you go back to lawn bowls."

Who knew old people's synchronized swimming was such a tough business?

Florence cleared her throat. "So, as I was saying, Mr Davenport, there's a spot for you. If you prove yourself."

Kathleen gave Grandpa Frank a nervous little wave. Grandpa Frank whispered to me, "Did she just say a place on *the team*? What have you got me into now, Frank?"

I got the distinct impression that he was not thrilled about joining an all-women's synchro team. I suppose I couldn't blame him. Florence *was* a bit scary.

Florence then glared at me from under her clumpy black eyelashes. "Am I right in understanding that you are here for moral support? As much as we'd love to have you, there's a minimum age requirement."

I said, "Yes, moral support, absolutely fine by me," because it *was* absolutely fine by me.

She gave a long blast on her whistle, which made everyone jump, and then trained her gaze on Grandpa Frank. "Come on then, Mr Davenport, let's see what you've got."

Even though Grandpa Frank didn't have the most streamlined of physiques and he'd shown no sign of it when he ended up in the pond, he was a surprisingly good swimmer.

He dived in with a little plop and didn't even make a splash. Then he lay on his back and followed the instructions which Florence barked from the side. He pointed his toes beautifully when he scissored his legs in the air. He also managed to twizzle about, with his arms held perfectly in position, like a wet and very hairy ballerina.

I think my favourite part was when he managed to do three forward rolls in a row. We all cheered when he bobbed to the surface and he seemed to enjoy the applause, even if his eyes were rolling about in his head from being so disorientated.

His awesomeness in the water surprised and delighted his seven potential teammates and Florence, who said Grandpa Frank was "a natural, with impeccable timing and a true flair for the sport". Whatever that means.

Florence even went as far as saying – in an almost threatening manner, come to think of it now – "There is nothing I wouldn't do to get an eighth member who is as talented as you. This team means everything to me. We have the nationals coming up and you could be our ticket to gold."

When the session was over, I was allowed in to have a try. Florence told me how to tread water, which was more like hard work than fun. I don't think I was the best pupil because she gave up pretty sharpish and

started going on to
Kathleen about how
to achieve proper
toe extension.

Grandpa Frank
paddled over to
me and then he
cupped his hands
together.

"Stick your foot
in there, Frank."

I did as I was told
and he catapulted
me straight up out
of the water. I went
so high I almost felt
like I was flying.
It was wonderful.
Until I hit the water
with an almighty
belly flop.

Which made Grandpa laugh and everyone else grimace and go, "Owwwww."

When we were climbing out the pool, Florence asked Grandpa Frank if he'd be signing up for the team.

He said, "Not really my thing," but I'd seen the size of his smile when Florence called him a star during their final practice of the Ariana Grande routine.

Later, after we had banged all the water out of our ears and had changed into our own clothes, he told me he used to be a pretty fast swimmer as a kid.

"Are you sure you don't want to give the team a go?" I asked.

He shook his head and said, "Water dancing at my age, don't think so!" but I noticed he'd folded up the registration form and slipped it into his pocket.

Outside on the leisure-centre steps, we bumped into Florence as she was heading for her car. I was a bit surprised that it was a blacked-out SUV. I had her down as the sort to drive one of those small grey cars that pootle about slowly, but that was probably because of her age and therefore wrong of me.

"Nice set of wheels, that," Grandpa Frank said.

"I know," Florence said as she climbed into the driver's seat. "I'd always wanted one and I always get what I want. No matter the cost."

The way she said that sounded a bit terrifying to me, but Grandpa Frank didn't seem concerned. All he said was, "Is that so?"

Then she said, "You will swim for me, Mr Davenport. I'll find a way to make you."

Again, this sounded a bit unnecessarily menacing to me. I half expected her to finish up with an evil cackling laugh, but she didn't, and Grandpa Frank just chuckled then gave her a wink.

When we got back to Autumnal Leaves it was really quiet because all the old people had fallen asleep, having tired themselves out playing virtual golf and riding mechanical bulls. Stephen asked us how our morning had been.

I said, "Good, actually, we've been swimming with **the Dolphins**."

Grandpa Frank trundled off into the lounge, saying, "Some of the best-looking dolphins I've ever seen. That Florence is something else."

I called after him, "See you in a couple of days for number four on the **Bucket List**."

He called back, "Can't wait."

And you know what? It really sounded like he meant it.

Stephen said, "Something's changed in that man. I swear I heard him singing in the shower this morning." Then he tilted his head and said, "Actual dolphins?"

"No, the glittery, old-lady kind."

I must have been smiling or something because he said to me, "You look like you are finding spending time with your grandfather very rewarding."

I said, "You know what? I am. **This is shaping up to be my best summer holiday ever**!"

And I realized I hadn't thought about the actual reward I'd be getting for looking after him for quite some time.

CHAPTER 26

Think twice before you trust someone whose smile doesn't sit right on their face

Even though it had turned out alright in the end, I said out loud to myself, "No more mess-ups, be thorough, Frank," when I set about organizing the next thing on the **Bucket List**. I remembered Grandpa Frank's words about preferring a non-water-based activity and I was scrolling through my options when Mum called up to me from downstairs.

When I got into the lounge, she and Dad were sitting at either end of the sofa. In the armchair opposite them was a man in an exceedingly shiny suit and a very dazzling smile which didn't sit right on his face.

Mum patted the cushion between her and Dad and

said, "Frank, come sit here. We want you to listen to what Mr Maloney has to say."

All three of them smiled at me as I sat down, but I didn't smile back. I wasn't stupid – I'd seen enough ambushes in films to know this was a heist.

Mr Maloney steepled his fingers together. "So, I hear you've been a very lucky boy."

I considered my situation for a moment and, apart from the money to spend on looking after Grandpa Frank, I found it hard to think of anything else that made me lucky. I had two parents who rowed all the time, a dad who was obviously up to something dodgy and no real friends to hang out with. Yeah, I was really lucky.

Mr Maloney pressed on. "The thing is, Frank, you've got something that doesn't belong to you."

They were all staring at me, but I wasn't about to say anything.

"And when things don't belong to you, you have to give them back."

The way he said it made it sound like I had done something really wrong and I couldn't let that go. "If

214

you're talking about the money, I can't give it back because it came from Grandma Nora, who *he* –" I pointed at Dad when I said that – "never told me about. And she's dead and you can't give a dead person their money back." I had him there.

Mum put her hand on my knee, but I moved my leg away. I didn't want her touching me. "Don't get yourself upset, Frank," she said. "We told you all along this would happen."

"No, Mum, I'm not giving it to you. I'm using it to look after Grandpa Frank. To make him happy. I've been taking him out and we've been having a good time together. He's not like Dad says. I mean, he can be a bit grumpy, but he's also alright, you know? No, he's more than alright."

"I thought I'd told you to stop seeing him," Dad said, very slowly.

"I know, but I didn't want to stop. And I'm glad I didn't."

"Well," Mum said, sitting up a bit straighter. "It's nice that you've had your fun with your grandpa, but now it's time for us to take control of the money and of him."

"See, the thing is," Mr Maloney continued, "that while the money has been left to you, it is perfectly legal for you to hand it over to your parents."

"Why would I do a thing like that? It's not for them. It's for giving Grandpa Frank his best life and I'm the one who Grandma Nora chose to do that."

Dad jumped to his feet and started pacing the room. "That man doesn't deserve a *best life*. I don't want you hanging out, getting to know each other. This whole thing is getting more than ridiculous now, Frank. You'll hand that money over to me because I'm your father and you'll do as I say. You hear me?"

"I won't! You'll only sink it into some stupid scheme that will end up with us broke or you in trouble with the police or getting beaten up or worse."

Mum took hold of my hand. "Your father won't do that. He's promised me."

I didn't believe a word of it, so I said, very sarcastically, "Well, if he's promised you, it must be true."

Mum ignored that. "We're planning to use the money to buy a new house somewhere. We'll start again. Get away from all the trouble. What do you think?"

I didn't know at the time what trouble she was talking about and, frankly, I was too cross to care. I pulled my hand out of hers and told her exactly what I thought. "I don't want to move! We haven't even been here a year yet. And there's *always* trouble. We came here to get away from trouble, but here it is again. And who's going to look after Grandpa Frank if I'm not here because *you've* moved us away again?"

Dad stopped walking about, threw his arms in the air and let out a long frustrated-sounding roar. "Will you stop going on about that man! I'm your father and, mark my words, you will do what I say."

I'd never seen him so angry. I didn't know at the time that it was because he was scared.

"I've got an appointment with the bank on Monday," he went on. "You can sign the money over to us then." He turned and marched out of the room like it was a done deal.

"I'm sorry your dad's so cross, Frank, but we are right about this. It's time to do the right thing," Mum said.

I ran upstairs to my bedroom, blinking back my

tears, because Davenport men don't cry. I sat down on my bed and breathed deeply so the emotions wouldn't overcome me. At that moment, I hated my parents. I hated them both. They only thought about themselves and nobody else – not Grandpa Frank, not me, just themselves.

But I wasn't like them. I had a responsibility to look after Grandpa Frank. To show him his best life. I didn't even care about the reward any more. I was doing it because *that* was the right thing to do. Because I wanted to. He was the only friend I had. The **Bucket List** might have been a bit of a daft idea to start with, but now, for reasons I couldn't fully explain, it meant something. I wasn't going to give up on it, or on Grandpa Frank.

It was only when I heard Mum showing that creep Maloney out that I had an idea.

She said, "Goodbye, Mr Maloney. We'll see you on Monday to get what's left of the money."

What's left of the money.

I couldn't exactly transfer any money over to them if there wasn't any.

I jumped up and got to work on my computer. I was going to spend it all. And I knew exactly what I was going to buy.

Once I'd booked the last **Bucket List** activities, I googled the number for J L Winterson solicitors and made a call to Mr Foster and told him what I wanted to do.

He said, "Are you sure?"

"I've never been surer."

Grandpa Frank and I were going to finish the **Bucket List**. There was no way I was going to let my parents stop that from happening.

CHAPTER 27

If you gotta cry, cry

I left before Mum and Dad woke up and got to Autumnal Leaves really early the next morning. Grandpa Frank was just heading out to fetch Dicky for his walk and, because he wasn't expecting me until the next day, he was surprised to see me.

He looked at my wheelie suitcase and said, "Are you moving in?"

"Yes, actually." And then, even though Davenport men don't cry, I did. "Sorry, don't think I'm soft. I'll pull myself together."

But Grandpa Frank said, "Don't you dare. You let it all out, son." And then he grabbed hold of me and gave me a hug, and I did as he said – I let it all out.

The whole time I was bawling, he didn't say anything, just patted me on the back and let me cry until I didn't need to cry any more.

When I was done, I let go and said in a wobbly, feeling-sorry-for-myself voice, "I can't remember the last time someone gave me a hug."

Grandpa Frank said, "Neither can I, son. Neither can I." Then he looked down at his shirt. "Blimey, Frank! How much snot did you have up that nose of yours?"

I laughed and a snot bubble burst out of my nostril to show him that the answer was *a lot*. Then, because I was a bit embarrassed about all the blubbing, I said, "I know I shouldn't cry, but I couldn't help myself."

"Why shouldn't you cry? I cried every day after Nora died. Only stopped when you showed up, with your hare-brained scheme of a **Bucket List**."

"You cried?" I *so* hadn't put Grandpa Frank down as the crying sort.

"Things are sad, you cry, you feel a bit better. It's not rocket science."

"Dad doesn't cry."

"Well, that's your dad and maybe if he did, he might feel a bit better too. Lord knows I've given him enough things to cry about. Now, that *is* something us Davenport men seem to be able to do – give their sons a reason to cry."

I wiped my nose with my sleeve. "You should talk to him."

"I know."

"Will you?"

"I'll try."

"I'm worried about him, Grandpa Frank."

"I haven't stopped worrying about that kid since the moment he was born. Now let's get your things inside. You can tell me what's going on while we pick up Dicky. And if you need a break from this **Bucket List** of yours, you must say."

"A break? No way. I've got activity four, five and six all planned out over the next two days."

We walked into the lobby and Grandpa Frank said to Stephen, in a way that made it sound like it had already been decided, "We've got a new resident staying with us."

I thought Stephen was going to have something to say about that, but he took one look at my face and said, "Shall I set up the relatives' guest room?"

I said, through a sniffle, "I'd rather stay in with Grandpa Frank, if you don't mind," because I didn't want to be on my own any more.

Stephen nodded decisively. "Then I'll set up a camp bed in Mr Davenport's room for you."

While we walked Dicky, I ignored the phone calls from Mum and Dad. I'd left before they'd woken up and they were wondering where I was. Where the money was, more like. I texted them to tell them I was staying at a friend's – which wasn't a lie – and not to worry, I'd be back after the weekend for the bank appointment on Monday. They seemed alright after that. I'd tell them I was moving out for ever later.

As we strolled around the park, I told Grandpa Frank about Dad turning up with a bloodied nose the other day, and about what had happened last night with Mr Maloney and Mum and Dad and that we were moving again. Even though he didn't really say anything other than "I see", I felt a bit better. Things would be alright, I reckoned, living at Autumnal Leaves. Especially now there was a proper games room.

We dropped Dicky off with Paul and Janice and then headed back to Autumnal Leaves. It was a good job I was there, because Grandpa Frank would have gone a really roundabout way to get back and we would have been late for activity four of the **Bucket List.** I think maybe he was distracted by the fact that Florence, the synchronized-swimming lady, had sent him three messages basically begging him to join her team.

I think he was tempted, but he said, "Can't really get on board with all those sequins, if I'm being honest, Frank."

Once we'd both had our travel wees, we took a cab to the station, then got a train up to London. Grandpa got himself comfy on one of the fold-down seats, pulled out a packet of chocolate Bourbons from his pocket and offered me one. "Tell me then, what death-defying scheme do you have in store for us on this fine Saturday?"

I stuffed a biscuit in my mouth and talked as I

munched. "I hope you don't mind, but this is actually something I've always wanted to do, but I think you'll like it too."

He said, "You think the other things we've done have been things I've always wanted to do?" and then he winked at me.

We met Akshan at the steps of the Royal Festival Hall and he gave us each some knee- and elbow-protectors as well as helmets, which neither of us wanted to wear, but Akshan insisted because he didn't want us falling on our heads and knocking ourselves stupid.

Grandpa nudged me. "Bit late for that, hey, Frank?"

Akshan, despite looking a bit like a grungy-cool-guy type, took his instructor role very seriously. He said, "**Parkour** is a fun and exciting sport but is not without its dangers."

Grandpa frowned. "Sorry, son, never heard of it."

I said, "What do you mean, you've never heard of it?"

"Parkour – never heard of it in my life."

Akshan explained. "Parkour is a training discipline

using movement that developed from military obstacle-course training."

"Sounds fantastic already," Grandpa Frank said flatly.

"The idea is to get from one point to another in a complex environment in the fastest and most efficient way possible."

Grandpa Frank screwed up his face. "Complex environment?"

"Built-up areas, like this one," Akshan said, gesturing around.

"I'll tell you what's a complex environment, the brain belonging to the fella who came up with this nonsense."

Akshan ignored Grandpa's muttering. "Parkour includes running, climbing, swinging, vaulting, jumping, rolling and crawling."

Grandpa said, "You're expecting me to climb, swing, vault and crawl? I'm older than I care to mention. And I'm certainly not a blinking monkey."

I said, "No, Grandpa, you're way better than a monkey."

He pulled a face at me. "Is that supposed to be some sort of compliment?"

It really was.

CHAPTER 28

There are times when you just have to attack

The first move Akshan tried to teach us was a basic landing. He said, "In parkour you are always taking drops and you've got to be ready for what the ground throws back at you."

Grandpa Frank turned to me and raised an eyebrow and I could tell he was thinking, *Would you listen to this guy!* I frowned at him to make him pay attention.

"You can't make a jump or leap without experiencing an impact," Akshan continued. "So if you want to fly, you have to be ready for the fall."

Grandpa Frank said, "I've heard it all now."

I gave him a little nudge, but I have to admit, it did

sound a bit like an inspirational meme.

Akshan then showed us how to jump and land correctly, which was basically jumping and bending your knees when you hit the ground. Grandpa Frank and I completely nailed this. We'd both jumped before.

It got more tricky for Grandpa Frank, though, when Akshan made us do it off a bench. Getting Grandpa up on it was the first hurdle, but after a couple of aborted attempts, he managed it. Once he was up though, well, you would have thought we'd asked him to jump off the top of Big Ben. I think because he was finding it a bit stressful, he got a bit narky.

"I don't see the point in this. When will I ever need to jump off a bench?"

"Now, Grandpa Frank," I said. "You need to jump off a bench now."

Akshan said, "It's a battle with your mind, not your body, Mr Davenport."

Grandpa Frank muttered something, but I heard what he said. He said, "I've enough blinking battles with my mind."

At the time, I didn't know what he meant by that, so

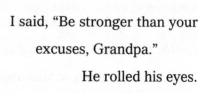

I said, "Be stronger than your excuses, Grandpa."

He rolled his eyes. "If I need a new hip after this, you're paying for it." But before I could ask how much one would cost, he jumped, and landed perfectly. Akshan and I both clapped, but we stopped quickly when he said, "Behave, would you? I only jumped off a bench," like he hadn't made a massive drama about it seconds before.

After we'd jumped off the bench ten times each, Grandpa said, "Excellent, well, that's parkour mastered. Shall we go and get a cup of tea and a meat pie?"

I said, "Meat pie later, we haven't even jumped over anything yet."

"Do I look like a racehorse?"

"No, Grandpa Frank, you do not look like a racehorse. You look more like a gorilla and I reckon gorillas would be excellent at parkour. Don't you think, Akshan?"

"Shall we move on to the next skill?" Akshan said in a tired-sounding voice.

I said, "Yes!"

Grandpa Frank said, "If we must."

Akshan walked us over to a low wall. He ran his hands over it like he was stroking a cat and whispered, "The wall," and then fell silent.

Grandpa Frank and I looked at each other and tried not to laugh. It got harder the longer Akshan carried on with the silent stroking. We both jumped when he suddenly spoke again.

"You have to be at one with your terrain to truly master parkour. Feel the landscape."

Grandpa Frank said, "Right you are," like he didn't think Akshan was right at all.

Akshan narrowed his eyes. "No, I mean actually *feel* the landscape." He grabbed our hands. "Here, you do it. *Feel the landscape.*"

Before we knew it, both Grandpa Frank and I were stroking the wall too. I can't say it's what I had in mind when I booked a parkour session. Not one of the YouTube videos I'd watched showed any parkour-ers stroking walls.

Grandpa Frank glared at me. "I'd rather be swimming with **the Dolphins**. In fact, I'd even rather be swimming with the Canada geese, given a choice."

After a minute or so of awkward wall-stroking, Akshan seemed satisfied we had felt the landscape sufficiently. "The next skill is the safety vault. It is a very important skill to master."

That sounded more like it. He demonstrated how to vault over a low wall with one hand and contact with one foot. It didn't look too tricky.

Grandpa Frank frowned deeply.

"Go on then, give it a go!" I said.

"You expect me to get my leg up and over there? Why wouldn't I just walk around it? You're having a laugh, sunshine."

I crossed my arms and nodded at the wall so he knew I wasn't having a laugh and wouldn't be feeling very sunshiny if he didn't at least give it a go.

"Sometimes, in life," Akshan said, calmly, "you can't go around things. Sometimes you have to attack them head-on."

Grandpa Frank gave me **the look** again, but this time he actually said out loud, "Would you listen to this guy?"

I was listening to him, and you know what? I was beginning to think Akshan had a point.

"Grandpa Frank, attack the wall. Attack it head-on. Attack it like you mean it."

"Calm down, I didn't say I wouldn't give it a go. But I'm going to need a run-up." He marched off quite some distance. For a moment I thought he'd pulled one over on me and was going to keep on walking until he reached a pie shop, but then he stopped and put both thumbs in the air. "Right, I'm ready to attack."

Akshan said to me, "I'm not sure he needs a run-up that big."

It turned out Akshan was right. We counted down from three and then Grandpa Frank began his attack, complete with battle cry. He started off quite fast, but it soon became obvious that he'd overestimated his stamina, because halfway to us he had to bend over, put his hands on his knees and catch his breath. But then he was off again, lumbering towards the wall. By the time his hand made contact he was pretty much at walking pace, but somehow he managed to get one leg up on it and drag himself over. It wasn't exactly elegant, but he'd done it and he was delighted.

"I'll be blown! I did not think I'd get myself over that."

I said, "You were brilliant!"

"Not sure when all this parkouring malarkey will ever be useful in real life though."

But he didn't know about what would happen later, on the roof of Grigsby's, and how useful his new-found skills would turn out to be.

CHAPTER 29

It's okay not to be okay

When we got back to Autumnal Leaves, I didn't think Stephen could have looked more surprised when he told Grandpa Frank that a woman called Florence had phoned and would he please ring her back about joining her synchronized-swimming team.

"She's persistent, I'll give her that," Grandpa said. But he didn't call her.

He then proudly showed Stephen the badge which Akshan had given him for completing introductory parkour training, and I realized I had been wrong about Stephen not being able to look more surprised, because he did.

It had actually been touch-and-go at one point whether Grandpa Frank was going to get his badge, because he'd had a right old grumble about learning to roll.

He'd said, "If you expect me to roll across the filthy streets of London, you've got another think coming."

But Akshan said, "No one gets through this life completely spotless."

Grandpa did this massive sigh and said, "Fine, I'll do it, if only to shut up Mother Teresa here," and he'd got on the floor and rolled about like an angry hedgehog.

I'd loved the parkour. Not so much the wall-stroking, but racing about and leaping over things had been awesome. It had made me forget about everything at home. It made me feel a bit free, if I'm being honest.

I was about to announce the next activity on the **Bucket List**, but the doors to reception opened and I saw a familiar face. Mum.

I was surprised to see Mum for two reasons. The first was that I hadn't expected her to find me. The second was that I hadn't expected her to look like a poodle wrapped in foil. Clearly, she'd been to Janice's for a "new do", because her hair looked weirdly blonde and floofy. She was also wearing her silver Puffa jacket – when Dad had first seen it, he'd said that she looked like she was ready to spend an hour and a half in the oven at two hundred degrees.

"Frank Davenport, what are you doing here?" Mum said.

Before I could answer, Grandpa Frank said, "I live here."

Mum was clearly not in the mood for clever remarks. She pointed at me. "I'm talking to him, Sherlock." Which I think was a dig about his hat.

Grandpa said, "Nice to see you, Tanya."

Mum did not say "Nice to see you" back, which was a bit awkward.

Stephen leaned forward and stretched his hand out over the desk. "It's so nice to meet some more of Frank's relatives. Would you like some tea in the lounge? I can arrange that for you."

I could tell by the look on Mum's face that she wanted to get a move on, but she gave Stephen's hand a shake anyway because she doesn't like looking as though she doesn't have any manners in public.

"No, thank you, I'm just here to get my son."

"He's such a wonderful boy," Stephen said, which I wasn't expecting and made me feel a bit nice but also a bit awkward so I just looked at the carpet.

Mum said, "He has his moments."

Dad walked in at this point, looking a bit flustered. "Tan, what's taking you so long?"

Mum folded her arms and looked at me. "Well, Frank, what do you have to say? You said you were staying at a mate's."

I remembered Akshan's advice about attacking things head on, so I said, "I am. I live here too now."

Dad did a little laugh, but he obviously wasn't finding anything funny. "I don't believe what my ears are telling me. Not a chance, kiddo. You're coming back with me and your mother."

"I'm not," I said. "I'm staying with Grandpa Frank. I've got my own camp bed and everything."

Dad stared at Grandpa Frank with this twisted half-smile on his face which was a bit unnerving. "This true?

You set him up with his own bed? Who do you think you are? No contact for well over a decade and now you think you can steal my son from me?"

Stephen looked a bit uncomfortable and scarpered at this point, saying, "I might just leave you folks to it. Besides, I must go, I promised to give Brenda a pedicure."

But no one was listening to Stephen. Grandpa Frank was glaring right back at Dad, and Mum was looking all hot and bothered in her tinfoil coat.

Grandpa Frank straightened up. "I'm not *stealing* your son, I'm the kid's grandfather."

Dad said, "Since when?"

"He was upset. Wasn't going to turn him away, was I?"

Mum said, "Frank's not upset, are you, Frank?"

But before I could tell her that I was, a bit, well, a lot, Dad said, "I know how to look after my own son," so I didn't actually get to answer the question. I don't think Mum really wanted an answer from me anyway.

Grandpa Frank said, "No one is saying you don't know how to look after your son. I just think it would do the lad good to have some space away from—"

"Away from *what*?" Dad said. "Away from his parents?"

Grandpa Frank didn't answer, but I did. "Yes, away from you two. You're doing my head in – both of you."

Mum said, "You *what*, young man?"

"You heard me. I'm going to stay here with Grandpa Frank." I did a big swallow after I said that, because Mum was looking like steam might come out of her at any point. If she was a roast poodle, she'd definitely be ready to come out of the oven.

Dad said, "Don't you talk to your mother like that. You're coming home with us."

I said, "You can't make me," even though I wasn't sure if that was true or not. But they'd have a hard time catching me, on account of all my new parkour skills.

Dad looked like he was going to say something but then his phone bleeped and suddenly he was more interested in that. He looked at the message and his forehead crumpled.

Mum said, "Who was that?"

Dad ignored her, put the phone back in his pocket and said to me, "I haven't got time for this. Frank, get in the car."

"No. I'm staying here. I need to look after Grandpa Frank."

He pointed at the door. "Frank. Car. Now."

I didn't move.

Grandpa Frank said, "I think we all need to calm down. Let the kid stay here for a few days."

"You are not going to tell me what happens, alright?" Dad snarled at Grandpa Frank. "You have no idea what's going on." Then he put his hands on his head and paced about the lobby. His face had gone really white.

Grandpa Frank ignored the snarling. "You in trouble, son?"

"What's it to you?"

Mum said, "Frank, what's going on? Who was that on the phone?"

"It was nobody, Tan," he said. But we all knew that was a lie.

Grandpa Frank took a step towards Dad. "If you're in trouble, let me help you."

"I don't want your help." Dad stopped pacing about and said to me, "I don't have time for any of this. You can have until Monday. Then you come back home and you do what you said you'd do." With that, he stormed out the doors and Mum chased after him.

They left me.

And even though I'd told them to, a tiny bit of me wished they hadn't.

Grandpa Frank and I stood there for a while, looking at the doors swinging back and forth. I didn't even know how I was feeling. Before I had a chance to figure out that I wasn't feeling that good – that I was miserable even – Grandpa Frank put his hand on my shoulder and said, "Come on, let's get you settled in."

I nodded because I didn't trust myself to speak without crying, and although I knew Grandpa Frank was okay with the crying thing, I didn't want to go overboard with it.

Grandpa Frank kept his hand on my shoulder all the way to our room. When he got to the door, he put his hand on the doorknob, but before he turned it, he said to me, "You have looked after me excellently, Frank John Davenport. Nora must have known what she was doing when she wrote her will. But right now, if you wouldn't mind, I'd like to look after you."

I took a bit of a gulp because my throat was full of feelings, but I managed to say, "I don't mind. I don't mind at all."

Then he said, "What on earth was going on with your mother's hair?"

I smiled. "I don't know. Do you know who she reminded me of?"

And at the exact same time we both said, "Patricia the poodle."

CHAPTER 30

You can ignore a problem, but it won't disappear

Grandpa Frank wanted to take a nap because his old bones were tired from hedgehogging around on the pavement all morning. While he snored away like a pneumatic drill, I wondered what I was going to do about Mum and Dad. Clearly, they expected me to hand over all the money which was supposed to be for looking after Grandpa Frank. They weren't going to be happy when they found out I'd spent it all. But it wasn't their money. It was mine.

I rang Mr Foster to check if he'd done as I'd asked.

He said, "Indeed I have. It's all gone through."

I'd spent every last penny. I hung up and let that

information sink in…but it didn't sink in very far, because Grandpa Frank woke up and did a massive yawn, which startled me out of my thoughts.

He looked at me and said, "Who are you and why are you in my room?"

I thought he was joking, so I laughed. "I'm your new roomie."

He kept staring at me so hard I thought his eyeballs might fall out. Then he said, "Get out. I didn't ask you in here. Why are you in here?" He almost sounded afraid.

"Grandpa Frank, calm down, it's only me, Frank. I'm staying with you for a while, remember?"

His eyes ran over my face a few times. "Frank? Why aren't you at school? Your mother will kill me if she finds out you've been playing truant and I knew about it."

"It's the summer holidays, Grandpa Frank."

He paused for a moment and his face seemed to relax back to normal. "The summer holidays. Of course. You're my grandson – Frank. I know that. I know that…" He wasn't speaking to me when he said that. He was speaking to himself.

Because I didn't understand at the time what was happening, and because I thought I was being funny, I said, "And he's back in the room!"

I wish I'd realized that he was lost. I wish I'd told him not to be scared and that I was there for him. But I guess people don't often say the right things at the right time.

He grabbed his hat from the end of his bed and said, in a bit of a cross voice, "Well, what are you waiting for? We'll be late for our tea."

I followed him out the door, delighted at the thought of food, because I was suddenly ravenous from all the parkouring and arguing. When we got to the lobby, Stephen was practically hopping from foot to foot in delight at the sight of three delivery men in beige outfits.

"Take it round the back, you can put it on the patio right by the wall. That way we won't be overlooked by people driving by."

"What's going on here then?" Grandpa Frank asked.

Stephen looked at me. "You know something about all this?"

"I'm guessing the SuperX8000 has arrived?"

Stephen ruffled my hair, the way Dad does, and said, "It certainly has."

"The what?" Grandpa Frank said.

"Only the best hot tub on the market, that's what!" Stephen said. "And this kid bought it for us."

Grandpa Frank didn't seem to share in Stephen's excitement. He pulled his hat further down onto his head and trundled off into the dining room, saying, "That's just what we need around here – a great big tub of bubbling geriatric soup."

He could say what he liked. I knew he'd be in there later, in his spangly pineapple swimming suit.

Over tea of boiled eggs and soldiers, Grandpa Frank tried to talk some more about the situation with my parents, but I wasn't really in the mood.

"What did your dad mean by *doing what you said you'd do* on Monday?"

I didn't want to admit to him that I'd promised to give away all the money, even if it had been a lie. And I didn't want to tell the truth – that I'd already gone and spent it all anyway – so I shrugged and said, "Nothing," and then began bashing one of my eggs with my teaspoon.

I must have gone a bit over the top, because he said, "Nothing quite as delicious as a pulverized egg, is there?"

I couldn't quite manage to smile.

Grandpa Frank pointed the end of his spoon at me. "This wallowing – it's not good for anybody. If you want to feel better, you're going to have to have a proper talk with your parents and let them know what's bothering you."

I sighed. "Do I have to? Couldn't we just do the next thing on the **Bucket List** instead?"

He tilted his head. "Absolutely! Ignoring a problem has always worked well for me." I knew he wasn't being serious, but then he sighed and said, "If it takes your mind off it for a while, let's do it – whatever ludicrous thing it might be. But don't be like me, Frank. Don't leave things too long."

"Alright, I'll speak to them," I said, but only so he wouldn't keep going on about it. I didn't have any intention of talking to Mum and Dad. There was no point, as they wouldn't listen. And besides, I was going to live at Autumnal Leaves with Grandpa and Stephen and Brenda and all the other oldies. I didn't need my parents.

Grandpa Frank stuffed a yolky soldier into his mouth. "Go on then, what delights do you have in store for us tomorrow?"

"You're going to **drive a monster truck** over a load of cars, up a ramp and through a ring of fire. According to the advert, it is going to be very exhilarating."

He didn't even blink before saying, "Standard activity for a Sunday."

Later that night, when I was lying on my camp bed, listening to Grandpa Frank's pneumatic-drill snoring again, I couldn't help but feel a bit sad. He didn't know it, but monster-trucking was going to be the very last activity on the **Bucket List**. There was no money left for anything else.

I took out the very grubby and crumpled piece of paper from my pocket and looked at the activities we wouldn't be able to do – like riding ostriches and swimming with sharks and wing-walking on planes – but missing out on those wasn't what I was sad about. The only thing left on the list that I wished I'd been able to do for him was my very last idea – to make Grandpa Frank and Dad friends again. But now I knew that wasn't going to happen, so I crumpled up the list and threw it in the bin.

CHAPTER 31

Your adrenal glands are actually located above your kidneys. Don't ask me where those are

When we left Autumnal Leaves the following morning, the hot tub was already full of old people. They'd decided to have their breakfast outside in the bubbles. When Brenda accidentally dropped her toast in, Grandpa Frank made some remark about geriatric soup now coming complete with croutons.

I had tried to convince Bruce, the owner of the monster truck, to pick us up in it, but he wasn't having any of it. Apparently, it is illegal to drive a monster truck down the A20. Luckily, Janice and Paul agreed to give us a lift in the dogmobile after we dropped Dicky back with them following his morning walk, so that was just as good.

Although I called it first, Grandpa Frank ignored the international rules of shotgun and clambered into the front passenger seat, saying, "Old bones get priority, kiddo."

As I buckled myself into the back with Dicky and Paul, Janice said, "Nothing like the sound of a 540 cubic inch Merlin engine to get the blood pumping and the heart racing, hey, Mr Davenport?" It turned out she was quite the monster-truck fan.

Grandpa Frank rolled his eyes. "My adrenal glands are twitching in anticipation." Despite his sarcastic tone and me not knowing what adrenal glands were, I took this to be a good sign.

It took us ages to get to the monster-truck arena, on account of all the traffic for the hot-air balloon show. I spent the journey trying to work out if I could feel my adrenal glands twitching too. I'd pinned their location down to either being somewhere in my stomach or behind my left nipple, near my heart. Janice, who was showing herself to be a bit of a petrolhead, used the car time to tell Grandpa Frank about the best ever monster-truck crashes, until he turned to her with a very ashen face and told her to leave it out.

When we finally arrived, Janice had got herself into a bit of a monster-truck frenzy. She told Paul he should miss his yoga session if he wanted so they could all stay and watch. It wasn't what Paul wanted. He said something about his chakras being all out of whack, but they ended up staying anyway.

Bruce met us in reception. He was only a little bit taller than me. I don't know why, but I had reckoned on a monster-truck driver being a big bloke, not a little guy with very well-kept fingernails and equally well-groomed eyebrows. Shows you how much I know.

"Blimey," he said, looking at Dicky, "that's a big dog."

I said, "We like big stuff. That's why we're here. Have we got your biggest truck? On the phone you said we could drive the biggest truck."

"Might have known you'd opt for the biggest," Grandpa Frank said.

"He friendly, is he?" Bruce asked nervously.

I looked at Grandpa Frank and answered honestly. "Most of the time. He does have his moods, but I think that's because he's getting on a bit."

Bruce said, "Not your grandfather, I'm talking about that dog," like it should have been obvious.

"Oh, yeah! Dicky's really friendly."

Grandpa Frank ruffled Dicky's ears. "He's the best dog in the world, is Dicky. Never puts a foot wrong."

That wasn't strictly true, but I didn't see any point in bringing up the bum-sniffing, pond-dipping incident.

Bruce was still eyeing Dicky suspiciously. To be fair, there wasn't that much height difference between them, so I could understand why he might have felt intimidated.

"So, do we have your biggest truck?" I said again, wanting to get going. "We want to be exhilarated."

Bruce nodded, not taking his eyes off Dicky. "She's ready and waiting for you... That really is a big dog."

I said "She?" because I'd asked for a truck, not some girl.

"Yes, Betsy's been waxed and polished, she has a full tank of fuel and her tyres are pumped and ready to whirl."

"Betsy's the name of the truck?" I said. "Don't you have something a bit more manly for us?"

Bruce's eyebrows did a little dance on his forehead. "You wait until you see her. She's a beast, is our Betsy. Her engine makes 1,450 horsepower!"

"That is a lot," I said. "How many alpacas do you think that would be?"

Bruce looked at me like he thought I wasn't being serious and then ignored my question. "Let's go and take a look at her, shall we?"

We followed Bruce into the arena, which was basically a huge dirt track surrounded by rows and rows of seats, with ramps and dirt hills and a line of old cars just begging to be jumped over.

Parked in the middle, all shiny and gleaming, was Betsy. Bruce hadn't been lying – she was a beast. She was the Dicky of the truck world. In fact, she was so massive, I could actually stand up under a wheel arch. She was yellow and red and had this huge grille on the front.

I think Grandpa Frank was impressed too, because he took off his hat and said, "Stick a match up my bum and set me on fire, what ungodly creation is that?"

"That is what you are going to be driving," I said.

255

He let out a low whistle. "Bit different to the Autumnal Leaves minibus." He was right about that.

Bruce asked for the stadium to be cleared in a very important-sounding voice. Janice didn't look like she was about to budge.

Bruce put on his crash helmet. "It's too dangerous to

be on the course. By all means stay where you are, if you fancy being flattened by five tonnes of metal and fibreglass."

Janice, Paul and Dicky moved pretty swiftly after that and went to sit on the fold-down stadium seats. Bruce then made me and Grandpa put on our helmets because, he said, "You need something to protect your skulls should we accidentally flip." And then fireproof suits, "In case the truck catches fire and we go up in flames."

He laughed after he said that, but Grandpa Frank didn't. In fact, he did that thing people do in church where they make the sign of the cross. I was all up for it though. How cool would it be to flip a monster truck? But then Bruce said, "It will all be fine if you follow my instructions. We're not going to do anything too crazy today," which was a bit deflating.

But little did he know.

CHAPTER 32

Don't believe the advertising

Once we were dressed in our helmets and suits, Grandpa Frank looked up at Betsy and said, "How do you think I'm going to get this crumbling body all the way up there?"

It was a reasonable question, because the doors were higher than our heads.

Bruce said, "Like this," and then he ducked under the truck and used the metal framework to pull himself up like a little monkey. I managed it, but even with his recent parkour training, Grandpa Frank needed a ladder to get him up and into the driver's seat.

Bruce and Grandpa Frank sat in the front and I

buckled myself into the back seat. Then I shouted in my best American accent, "Let's get truckin'! If the mud ain't flyin', you ain't tryin'!"

Janice whooped from the stands, but Bruce and Grandpa Frank both turned around and looked at me like I'd put my helmet on backwards.

"*What?*" I said. They weren't going to dampen my enthusiasm. "Rev your engine, Grandpa Frank! Let's see what Betsy can do!"

"What Betsy can do first," Bruce said, "is drive off in a slow and controlled fashion in first gear."

I'd seen enough videos on YouTube to know that didn't sound very monster-trucky. But when Grandpa Frank turned the key in the ignition, Betsy let out an almighty growl, which was very exciting.

Janice, who was now standing on her seat, yelled, "That's the sound of 1,450 horsepower right there."

"Or 4,350 alpaca!" I shouted back, because I already knew that one horse was worth three alpaca, give or take (and I'd done the maths on the calculator on my phone, before you think I'm some genius).

Grandpa Frank slid the gear stick into first gear and

Bruce said, "Good, good, easy does it," and we began to crawl forward.

"Easy does it" was not what I had expected to hear when I booked a monster-truck experience. Grandpa Frank clung onto the steering wheel like it was a life buoy, and we crept around the arena at twelve miles an hour, as though Betsy was powered by a single elderly alpaca.

"Can't you go a little faster?" I asked. "This is not the exhilarating experience I imagined."

Bruce shot me down pretty quickly. "Safety before exhilaration. It is important that your grandfather and Betsy have secured an understanding. He needs to know how to handle her before we try any tricks."

"Tricks?" That sounded more like it. "What tricks?"

"Just you wait," Bruce said. "Are you ready to move into second gear, Mr Davenport?"

Second gear did not count as a trick in my book.

Grandpa Frank said, in a very serious-sounding voice, "I am," and then he moved the gear stick.

"Good, good, a little more throttle," Bruce said.

"How about a lot more throttle?" I said.

Grandpa Frank pushed down on the accelerator and the speedometer sprang all the way up to sixteen miles an hour. I slumped down on the back seat as we eventually completed another lap of the stadium. If we'd been racing Brenda in her new top-of-the-range wheelchair, I would have put my money on her to win.

"You having fun back there?" Grandpa Frank yelled over his shoulder.

I said, "Yup, heaps," but I think wherever my adrenal glands really were, they'd shrivelled up and died.

Four laps later, I'd stopped paying any interest to what was going on and was leafing through *Monster Mag*, which I'd found on the back seat. There was an article on a truck called the Raminator. Now that was a manly name. The Raminator was the fastest-known monster truck. Its top speed was 99.1 miles per hour. Betsy was currently travelling at 23 miles per hour. So disappointing. I only looked up from the magazine when Grandpa Frank turned off the ignition.

"You're ready," Bruce was saying, "to move on to the next level of training."

I think an adrenal gland twitched at that. Maybe "next level" meant flying through flaming hoops.

He pointed at the tiniest mound of earth at one end of the arena. "You're going to drive up that hill—"

"And take off and fly through the fiery hoop of fury?" I asked.

"And drive down the other side in a slow and controlled manner."

I did the biggest sigh I could so Bruce would know I was not feeling very exhilarated. "Couldn't he try driving up that bigger one over there?"

Bruce laughed and shook his helmeted head. "Absolutely not! That's for professionals and, besides, how old is your grandfather – like, over eighty? There's no way I'm letting an eighty-year-old attempt that."

I thought the age comment was going to land Bruce in a whole heap of trouble, but Grandpa Frank didn't respond. He did what he was told and drove up one side of the tiny hill in a slow and controlled manner. And then he drove down the other side in a slow and controlled manner. It didn't even give me the tummy flutters.

"Hey, not bad at this monster-trucking, am I?" Grandpa Frank said.

I said, "Yeah, you're nailing it," so as not to hurt his feelings, but I don't think Grandpa Frank had a proper idea what monster-trucking was all about.

Before Grandpa Frank could drive up the hill again, a voice came over the tannoy system, saying, "Bruce, can you come to reception? There's some woman here causing a fuss."

Bruce told Grandpa Frank to turn the ignition off. "I'd better go deal with this." He pointed a finger at me and said, unnecessarily sternly, considering I was a paying customer, "No trying to get your grandfather to drive through fiery hoops."

After Bruce had climbed down and disappeared through the arena tunnel towards reception, Grandpa Frank turned to me and said, "He might have said no fiery hoops, but he didn't say anything about that massive mound over there."

"What are you saying?"

"I'll show him what an eighty-year-old can do." He winked at me and then turned the ignition back on. "Can't see any harm in a slow and controlled drive up and down that mound, can you?"

Despite the lack of hoops and flames, I was properly thrilled by his suggestion. I said, "I can't see any harm at all," because I couldn't.

I probably should have looked a bit harder.

Grandpa Frank did one lap of the arena and we waved at a surprised-looking Paul and Dicky and a fiercely-excited-looking Janice, who was giving us a double-handed rock-on salute.

When we squared up in front of the mound, it looked

a LOT bigger than I'd first thought. It was about ten times the height of the hill Grandpa Frank had practised on. I probably should have told him to take it in a slow and controlled fashion, but I wanted to treat my adrenal glands, so instead I said, "You're going to need a lot of juice to get up that. Pedal to the metal and make this baby fly!"

"There won't be any flying," Grandpa said, incorrectly as it turned out. "We're going to go up and then down the other side, that's all."

It wasn't what I wanted to hear but I said, "Fine – get going, though, before Bruce gets back."

Grandpa Frank gripped the wheel, slammed his foot down and Betsy lurched forward with a huge growl. It was only once we were at the top that we both realized the problem. And the problem was, it wasn't a mound – it was a ramp. And there was no other side, just a massive drop. We didn't drop though, we flew up, up, up into the air!

CHAPTER 33

It's not always the big bumps in the road that catch you out, it's the little ones too

If you want to try and slow down time – which, if you're as old as Grandpa Frank, might seem a good idea – I suggest soaring through the air in a monster truck. It's amazing really. We can't have been airborne for all that long, but I can remember *everything*.

I remember everything Grandpa Frank said, which was a whole lot of unrepeatable words. I remember the look on his face – until he covered it with his hands. I remember seeing the steering wheel and thinking *Someone really ought to have hold of that*. I remember the flash of silver catching my eye and realizing Mum was there in the stands, with her Puffa jacket and poodly hair. I remember knowing that my adrenal glands were definitely located in my bum.

And then I remember the landing.

Because we weren't exactly level – and for that I blame Grandpa Frank for letting go of the steering wheel – we didn't land on Betsy's two back wheels, like I'd seen trucks do in all the YouTube clips. We landed on one. This meant we tipped a bit to one side. And when I say a bit, I mean a lot. Luckily, Grandpa Frank reacted and pulled the steering wheel to right us. But he went a bit too far and we ended up bouncing over to the other side. He swung it back the other way, but it was too much of a correction again and we tipped back to the left. So he pulled it again and... well, you can see where this is going. We bobbled about from side to side, dirt flying up around us, while Grandpa Frank shouted a load of words which would have to have been bleeped out if we'd been on telly.

I don't think either of us knew how it was going to play out. At that moment, flipping Betsy didn't seem quite such an exhilarating idea. Luckily, Grandpa

Frank's furious steering started to work, and the bobbling became a bit less bobbly.

He said to Betsy, "Steady there, girl. Steady there, girl," and she started to do as she was told. Soon, we had four wheels on the dirt and smiles of relief on our faces.

Bruce and Mum didn't look so smiley though.

I leaned out the window and waved. "Don't worry," I said confidently. "We've got it all under control."

Then, just as Grandpa Frank was shouting out to Bruce, "This old man just slayed it!" he clipped the teeny hill he'd driven up earlier with a front tyre.

Suddenly Betsy was upside down and airborne again. Which was both surprising and embarrassing, considering the "slaying it" comment.

Just as soon as Betsy was up in the air, she was landed down on her back in the dirt.

But then she **bounced** up again.

Then **dropped** down again.

Then a smaller **bounce** up.

Then another **thud** down.

Then she just **lay** there.

And we just **sat** there, strapped into our seats and

looking at our feet, which were now above our heads.

It took a few moments before we were able to speak. Eventually, Grandpa Frank turned off the engine and said, "Enough exhilaration for you, Frank?"

I said, "I think we're ready for the flaming hoop of fury."

Grandpa Frank said, "I think I'm ready for a pint."

We unbuckled our seat belts and climbed out of one of Betsy's windows. Her wheels were still whirling, like a tortoise trying to right itself. It made me feel a bit sorry for her.

Grandpa Frank shook his head. "Lesson there, lad. It's not always the big things in life that can tip you up and set you on your backside."

Everyone came rushing over to us, shouting.

Paul said, "Are you okay?"

Janice said, "That was awesome."

Bruce said, "Don't tell anyone I left you alone with the keys."

Mum said, "I thought you were dead!" which I personally think was a bit overdramatic – but that's Mum for you.

She pulled my helmet off in a not-very-gentle manner, grabbed hold of my head and then began examining me from top to toe for injuries. When she was satisfied I still had all my arms and legs, she began planting these big lipsticky kisses all over my face. Before I could tell her to pack it in, she pulled me in for a big hug and said into my hair, "Frank, don't you ever do that to me again. You're just too precious."

I wasn't about to get back in a monster truck any time soon, mainly because I didn't have the money to, but I didn't tell her that. I was too busy feeling precious.

And remembering what hugging her felt like.

I think she would have hugged me for ever if Dicky hadn't lumbered up and started sniffing her bum. I guess, what with her new hairdo, Dicky had also noticed she had a passing resemblance to Patricia the poodle.

The interruption must have reminded Mum why she was there, because her face suddenly got all tight and scared-looking.

I said, "Mum, what's the matter?"

She looked over at Grandpa Frank, who was putting his deerstalker back on, and said in a shaky voice, "Mr Davenport, I need your help."

Grandpa Frank didn't hesitate. He said, "Then you shall have it."

I could sense something bad must have happened, so I said, "Mum, what's going on?"

Mum swallowed hard. "Your dad's gone missing. He's in trouble, Frank. Serious trouble."

And I felt like I was upside down and spinning through the air all over again.

CHAPTER 34

London traffic is a nightmare

Grandpa Frank walked Mum over to one of the fold-down seats and said, "Tanya, tell us exactly what you know."

"One minute, Frank was pleading with someone on the phone. The next, a car had pulled up outside the house and he was gone. I tried calling, but he didn't pick up. Then I got this text an hour later saying to bring the money to Grigsby's by 2 p.m. if I wanted to see Frank again."

"What money?" Grandpa Frank asked.

Mum looked at me and said, "They want two hundred grand."

"Who's Grigsby?" Grandpa Frank asked.

Mum shook her head. "Not a person – the supermarket."

"That's quite some grocery shop they're intending," Paul said, but then Janice nudged him and he shut up.

"Frank," Mum said, "I know you have your reasons for keeping the money Nora left you, but you have to hand it over. You don't want to see your dad hurt or worse, do you?"

"No, of course not," I said, because I absolutely did not want that.

She stroked my cheek. "You're a good boy, Frank."

I didn't feel like a good boy and, because she looked so desperate, I couldn't even tell her that the money was gone.

Grandpa Frank put his deerstalker back on and got practical.

"Did you phone the police?" he asked.

"How could I? They're not going to be interested in helping us and, besides, I won't have Frank ending up in trouble with the law."

Grandpa Frank checked his watch. "It's almost

1 p.m. We need to get going if we're going to save my son."

"What are you going to do?" I asked.

"I don't know yet, but whatever it takes. I will not let anything happen to him. We just need to get to him."

Janice made for the exit, saying, "Everybody into the dogmobile!"

Grandpa Frank helped Mum up from her seat. I saw her squeeze his hand and whisper, "Thank you."

He gave her the tiniest nod and said, "Thank you," back. At the time I didn't know why he was thanking her. Now I think it was because she had gone to him for help. I guess everyone wants to be needed.

It was a bit of a squeeze in the back of the dogmobile, especially because Dicky would not leave Mum alone. He was climbing all over her, sniffing her ears, waggling his tail in her face and licking her arms. Another time I would have found it funny to tell her it was because she reminded him of Patricia the poodle, but at that moment all I could think about was the money I didn't have. That I'd already spent Dad's ticket out of trouble.

Janice must have been inspired by the monster-trucking, because she drove like an absolute maniac. Way worse than Mum. She didn't take any notice of roundabouts and drove right over the top of them, letting other road users know she was coming by holding her hand down on the bark-horn.

"At least we're making good time," she said when Paul began whimpering about traffic lights being there for a reason.

And Janice was right, we were making good time – until she swung a left and we ended up stuck in a whole heap of traffic. Janice kept her hand on the bark-horn as though it might make all the other vehicles disappear. Unsurprisingly it didn't work, but it did make the atmosphere inside the car even more intense.

Grandpa Frank, who was sitting in the front, removed Janice's hand from the horn, checked his watch again and said, "Don't panic, there's still time," but his voice wasn't all that convincing.

Mum said, "Can someone get this dog out of my face? I've just got a text."

She read it out loud. *"Don't forget – 2 p.m., top floor, Grigsby's car park."* She dropped her head into her hands. "What is it with your father and the top floor of car parks? First Waysafe in Woking, now here!"

The people in the cars in front of us started turning off their engines. Grandpa Frank wound down his window and called out to a man who was leaning against his car, having a cigarette.

"You know what the hold-up is?"

"Backed up for miles. No one's going anywhere for a while. Hot-air balloon's gone down on the dual carriageway. Took off from a field over there apparently."

"That's it then," Mum said and started to cry.

I felt my chin start to wobble too, but then Grandpa Frank said, "That's most certainly not *it*! Follow me. I have an idea." And before my chin could get really involved with the wobbling action, he was off.

We all climbed out of the dogmobile and weaved in and out of the traffic after Grandpa Frank. He was racing away, his deerstalker ear-flaps flapping about madly. He'd never keep up that pace. If his idea was to run the eight miles to Grigsby's, it wasn't a good one.

Luckily, he had a better idea than that. A much better idea.

CHAPTER 35

Don't meet people on car-park roofs if you owe them money

After a bit more traffic-weaving, Grandpa Frank hit the pavement and we followed him up over a bridge, through a gap in a fence and into a sports field. A sports field that was packed full of hot-air balloons preparing to take off.

"Look out for Balloon Dave," he shouted to me.

I knew then what his idea was. He was going to catch a flight to Grigsby's.

I spotted Balloon Dave's rainbow-coloured balloon, half-inflated, in the far corner. "He's over there!" I shouted and Grandpa Frank was off running and ear-flapping again.

When we reached Dave, Grandpa Frank bent over, put his hands on his knees and just about managed to say, "We need your balloon."

Balloon Dave said, "But I need my balloon."

I said, "It's an emergency, we need to save my dad from being thrown off the top storey of the Grigsby's car park."

Balloon Dave frowned like he didn't believe me, but Mum, Janice, Paul and Grandpa Frank all said, "It's true!"

Balloon Dave folded his arms. "Where's my balloon come into it?"

I'd thought that was obvious, but I said, "You're going to fly us there."

"I'm not driving the number 363 – I'm a hot-air balloon pilot, and we rely on the direction of the wind currents. I can't just choose where the balloon goes."

I said, "What, *really*?"

"Yes, really!"

It's a wonder the things are even allowed in the air.

Mum said, "Do you think the wind currents will take us to Grigsby's?"

281

Balloon Dave licked his finger and stuck it in the air. Then he looked at some app on his phone and said, "You know what, they might."

Mum took his hand in hers and said, "Please, I beg you," and then she shook her poodly hair, which, for some reason, seemed to do the trick.

"Okay, get in. Don't let it be said that Dave Bobbins is the type of man who would see another man be thrown off a car-park roof."

"You're a hero," Mum said.

Balloon Dave blushed and said, "I needed to pick up some milk anyway."

We all clambered into the balloon basket – the biggest in the county, which was lucky because there were a lot of us and Dicky took up a fair amount of space. Balloon Dave shut the door, cranked up the flames, the balloon inflated fully, and we were off.

During the flight, I kept trying to find a way to tell Mum that I didn't have two hundred grand, but each time I opened my mouth, the words got lost. Even now, I don't know what I thought was going to happen when we were face to face with Dad's captors.

Because of all my worrying and thinking, I didn't know how long it took to get to Grigsby's, but I did know we didn't have much time left by the way Grandpa Frank kept checking and rechecking his watch. We were quite high above the car park as we approached, but I could make out three people on the roof.

"I'm bringing her down," Balloon Dave said, and he began to ease off the gas.

As we dropped lower, the people on the roof started pointing up at us. All except one, who had his hands tied behind his back.

"Dad!" I shouted. "There he is." He didn't wave because he couldn't.

Balloon Dave said, "I don't fancy my chances of landing it on there. Too many cars."

"Just get as close as you can," Grandpa said. "I'll jump the rest."

My eyes must have been as big as balloons when I said, "But, Grandpa, you only just about managed to jump off a bench, how are you going to manage to jump out of a balloon with your crumbly old body?"

"Who said I have a crumbly old body?"

"You did, like, heaps of times!"

Balloon Dave said, "I'll get you as close as I can, but it will still be a bit of a drop. Are you sure you want to do this, Mr Davenport?"

"Never been more certain of anything in my life. My boy needs me." He turned to me and winked. "What was it that Akshan said? If you want to fly, you have to be ready for the fall?"

"Something like that," I said. "But I'm not convinced he was thinking of eighty-year-olds leaping out of hot-air balloons."

"If I don't jump out of this balloon, I'll live to regret it, and I already have too many of those. Any impact I experience from the ground isn't going to hit me as hard as the impact of letting my son down again."

To be honest, it didn't feel like the right time for a deep-and-meaningful, what with my dad seconds away from being dangled over the pavement, so I said, "Smashing, I'll count you down, then give you a shove if you bottle it."

As Balloon Dave brought us down lower and lower, we could tell there was a bit of a commotion going on

285

below. The two men were shouting at Dad, "It's the police! You called the police?" They didn't sound happy.

Clearly, we weren't the police. We were a pensioner in a Sherlock Holmes hat, a woman who looked like a poodle wrapped in tinfoil, a couple of dogmobile-driving tri-business owners, a massive dog with a bum-sniffing problem, a balloon pilot who wasn't the sort of man to let another man be thrown off a car-park roof... and a kid who was about to let his whole family down.

CHAPTER 36

My Grandpa Frank is awesome

Balloon Dave was doing a brilliant job of getting us lower. From our position, we could hear what Dad's captors were saying quite clearly. Because they couldn't see us from below, they were still convinced that we were the police and they weren't thrilled about it.

The big guy with the long straggly ponytail – the one I'd seen getting out of Dad's car in the tennis-club car park – was pushing Dad towards the edge of the roof, saying, "So, Frank Davenport, it seems your face is going to be meeting the pavement very soon now."

Dad tried to reason with him by saying, "When's the last time you saw the plod rock up in a rainbow-coloured hot-air balloon? It will just be from that balloon show."

Ponytail wasn't persuaded. "Could be an undercover job."

Dad said, "Oh yeah, a massive balloon is very undercover. Who's going to notice that hovering by Grigsby's?" I had to give it to him, Dad wasn't the politest of hostages, despite being inched towards the edge of the roof.

The other guy said, "He's got a point, Mr Kay."

Even from way up in the basket, by the way he spoke and the way he moved, I knew who it was. It was Tony.

I said, "Mum, that's your tennis coach down there."

Mum's mouth opened really wide. "What's he doing here?"

The balloon dropped a bit lower and Balloon Dave said, "That's as close as I can get you. You'll have to be quick, the air current could change direction at any time."

Grandpa Frank poked his head over the side of the basket to have a look. We were about three metres above and one metre away from the car park. It doesn't sound much, but believe me, if you had to jump it, you'd think otherwise.

When Mr Kay saw Grandpa, he shouted, "It's not the rozzers. It's Sherlock-blinkin'-Holmes!"

Dad stammered, "Er…that's my dad actually."

And Mr Kay said, "Your dad is Sherlock Holmes? Give over!"

"No," Dad said. "My dad is Frank Davenport and for some reason he's climbing out of a hot-air balloon."

At this point Grandpa Frank had one leg either side of the basket and he was readying himself to jump. He said, "Hang on, son. I'm coming to get you."

Dad didn't sound that pleased to see him. He said, "What are you doing, you old fool? Get yourself back in that balloon."

"Come to think of it, he looks too old for Sherlock Holmes," Mr Kay said.

Dad said, "He's not Sherlock Holmes, there is no such person as Sherlock Holmes. That's just a crazy old man in a deerstalker hat."

Either the "old" comment or the "crazy" comment

must have triggered something in Grandpa Frank because, before we knew what was happening, he jumped. It took us all by surprise. I didn't even get to do a countdown.

He used all his parkour expertise and landed perfectly, bending his knees to lessen the impact and slowing his forward momentum by doing one of his hedgehog rolls – right into Tony, knocking him off his feet. It was amazing.

Grandpa Frank stood up, readjusted his hat and said, "I'm here to discuss the release of my son."

The balloon started to rise up and away, so I leaned over the side and shouted, "He isn't Sherlock Holmes. He's way better than Sherlock Holmes. He's my Grandpa Frank and he's awesome!"

Dad yelled, "Cor blimey, Frank, what do you think you're doing up there? Wait till your mother hears what you've been up to." Which was a bit rich coming from him, considering he was the one being held hostage.

Mum appeared next to me and said, "Hello, *Frank*," in her *I'm not happy with you* voice.

Dad must have known he was in the doo-doo,

because his voice came out all stammery when he said, "Alright, Tan, my angel?"

Mum had to really shout because the balloon was getting higher and higher. "Well, you've really gone and done it this time, haven't you? Two hundred blinking grand! And getting yourself kidnapped for the second time, and on a car-park roof of all places. What did I tell you after the last time?"

"You said no more car-park roofs, my treasure. But I didn't really get a choice – Mr Kay chose the location."

Balloon Dave turned off the gas and we must have picked up another air current, because we headed back towards them. We were able to hear Mr Kay say, "When it comes to conducting a convincing negotiation, a car-park roof has obvious logistical advantages."

Grandpa Frank took a step forward and said, "So let's negotiate."

Mr Kay raised an eyebrow. "You've got the cash?"

"We can get it," Grandpa Frank said and looked up at me. "Isn't that right, Frank?"

And I said, "Oh right, yes, about the money…"

But before I could explain, Balloon Dave said, "Another strong air current!" and the balloon swept up and away from the car-park roof.

CHAPTER 37

No one can agree on the best parking space

Grandpa Frank, Dad, Tony and Mr Kay got smaller and smaller as we floated away, and Mum got angrier and angrier.

She said, "Take us back immediately. We can't leave those two on their own to sort this mess out."

Balloon Dave said, "I don't control the weather, love."

Mum didn't think that was a good enough excuse. "You land this balloon on that car-park roof or I'll do it myself, *love*."

That worried me, because Mum has trouble driving a car, let alone piloting a hot-air balloon.

Dicky must have caught on to the fact that Mum wasn't happy, so he decided to lend his support to her argument by putting his front paws up on Balloon Dave's shoulders and growling.

Janice and Paul tried to pull him off, but he wasn't having any of it. Eventually, Balloon Dave gave in and said, "Okay, I'll give it a go, but call your dog off."

Mum said, "Down, big dog," and Dicky got down and wiggled in next to her.

Balloon Dave fiddled about with the gas and we went up, then down, then drifted even further away from the car park. Then he took us up really high and said, "I'll try that again."

Mum said, "Come on, we haven't got all day. That's my family down there and I refuse to watch them in trouble as you piddle about with your hot-air balloon."

Balloon Dave looked like he might give her a piece of his mind, but she gave him one of her *I'm not messing about* stares and Dicky growled, so he turned back to his balloon-piddling.

Soon we were smack bang over the roof of the car park, and we were heading down. Mum said, "That looks like a good space, between the red Ford and the blue Peugeot."

"Or the one by that transit van?" Janice suggested.

Paul pointed out another space next to a blacked-out Hummer, but Mum said, "No, the BMW on the other side has parked on the wonk, he won't get in there." Then she said, "Well, pick one, Dave! There are plenty to choose from and you're just driving around aimlessly."

Balloon Dave shouted a bit when he said, "Again, I don't control the air currents. This thing is going to land where it wants to."

It so happened that it landed in the space Mum had originally suggested.

I think, by the look on Balloon Dave's face, he was expecting some kind of applause, but he wasn't getting that from Mum. She just said, "*See*, that wasn't so hard, was it?"

Mum and I left Dave, Janice, Paul and Dicky and jumped out of the basket, crawled out from under the canopy and raced over to Dad and Grandpa Frank. Mr Kay and Tony had been joined by two other men, who looked enough like Mr Kay for me to guess they were his relatives.

Mr Kay cracked his knuckles and said in a threatening voice, "So which one of you—"

But Mum cut him off by shouting, "Frank James Davenport! You want to tell me *now* what all this is about?"

Dad, who still had his hands tied behind his back and was being held onto by Tony, looked at the floor and scuffed his shoe about. "It all got a bit out of control, Tan. The money that I borrowed from them before, well, the interest on it built up and up and the amount grew and grew – I knew I could never pay it back. I thought they wouldn't find me when we moved, but they tracked us down. You never won a membership to the tennis club, it was all a ruse to get to me. If you hadn't—"

"Don't you dare pin this on me, Frank! I swear I'll—"

Mr Kay interrupted at this point. "Can someone explain why I'm listening to a family domestic? I'm conducting a—"

But Mum held up her hand and cut him off again.

"Er, excuse me," she said rather hotly. "I'm trying to have a word with my husband."

Tony said, "I should let Mr Kay speak, if I were you."

Mum said, "Oh, and don't even get me started on you! Go back to whatever sunbed you crawled out of!"

The two Mr Kay-looking men sniggered at that.

Tony said, "Boss, you going to let her speak to me like that?"

"I should have known you weren't a real tennis coach when you told me that a tie is solved by players arm-wrestling," Mum went on.

So at least that explained why she was still so horrible at tennis.

Mr Kay said, "Can everyone just shut up and let me work out if anyone is going for a flying lesson off this roof today. Now, you said the *kid* is the one with the money?"

Grandpa Frank pulled me into him and said, "He doesn't have it on him, but we can get it, we just need to go to the bank. You have my word."

Mr Kay fixed me with a stare. "This true, kid? You've got two hundred thousand quid you can get to me?"

Everybody was looking at me and waiting for me to answer. I knew what I had to say wasn't going to go down well.

"So?" Mr Kay said. "Do you?"

Grandpa Frank gave me a little nudge. "Go on, Frank. Tell him you're good for the money. We've had our fun, I don't need my villa in Spain, we need to help your dad now."

I swallowed hard and looked my dad in the eyes and said, "I'm sorry, I didn't know you'd need it. I haven't got it."

"What do you mean, you haven't got it?" said Mum, Dad and Grandpa Frank all at once.

I swallowed even harder. "I've spent it."

I was right, that little revelation didn't go down well. In fact, it went down like a lead hot-air balloon.

CHAPTER 38

There is no way out of
some situations

I felt very exposed standing up there on Grigsby's roof, with everybody looking at me. I felt like I'd let everyone down – Mum, Dad, Grandpa...I even felt a teeny bit bad for Mr Kay, because he looked so disappointed about the sudden lack of cash coming his way.

I could tell Mum was trying not to sound too angry when she said, "You'd better not be joking around right now, young man."

Dad said, "He'd better be."

"I'm sorry," was all I managed to say. "I thought I was doing the right thing."

"But what did you spend it on?" Mum asked. The anger had floated out of her voice and been replaced by something much worse, and that was despair.

I decided I may as well be honest, so I took a deep breath and told her. "A limo ride, some taxis, a hot-air balloon flight and I rented Dicky. An experience swimming with the old-lady-dolphins and a parkour lesson with Akshan. A go at monster-trucking and a new wheelchair for Brenda. A virtual tennis game and virtual golf, a bucking bronco and a dance game – oh, and a hot tub."

Mum blinked twice but didn't say anything.

Dad looked over at the edge of the roof and said, a little desperately, "That's a lot of stuff, Frank, but it can't add up to **£462,000**. There must be some left."

"There'd better be some left," Tony said, giving Dad a bit of a shove.

I shook my head. "I bought something else too."

"There's more? What else could you possibly need after all that?!" Dad said.

"I bought Autumnal Leaves."

"You did what!?" Mum shouted.

"I bought the old people's home."

"I know what Autumnal Leaves is, what I don't know is why you, an eleven-year-old boy, would want to buy it? What are you going to do with a building full of pensioners?"

I took a deep breath so I could get everything I wanted to say out. "I bought it because I'm going to live there. I want to stay with Grandpa Frank and look after him because I'm good at it and I enjoy it and he's my only friend and that place feels like the nearest thing to a home that I've ever had."

Dad said, "I've never heard of anything so ridiculous."

"Grandpa Frank is my family now and I'm not going to walk out on him. You're the one who said you don't walk out on family."

Grandpa Frank squeezed my shoulder. "Oh, Frank, I don't know what to say."

Dad didn't seem to know what to say either, because he spluttered, "Well, when I said family, I...I...well, you know what I meant...not him."

I couldn't believe what I was hearing. "Grandpa Frank just jumped out of a hot-air balloon for you!"

Dad said, "I never asked him to."

Mr Kay rubbed his hands over his face and said, in a weary-sounding voice, "So am I understanding this correctly – there is no money?"

I shook my head.

"Seems you're leaving me no choice..." Mr Kay looked over at Tony and the other two men and nodded.

I said, "No, please don't! I'll get the money, I promise!"

"Heard that one before, kid," Tony said and pushed Dad a step closer to the edge of the roof.

I looked up at Grandpa Frank and said, in a very panicky voice, "Grandpa Frank, what do we do?"

But before he could answer, Mum had launched herself at Tony, which took us all by surprise. She shouted, "If anyone's going to throw my husband off a roof, it's going to be me!"

I don't think she really meant that, but the stress of the situation must have got to her. Anyway, she went low – below the knees – and took Tony clean out. It made me think she was wasting her time on the tennis – she should look into rugby.

Dad tried to wiggle away. What with his arms still

being cable-tied behind his back, he looked a bit like a terrified caterpillar scooching along the ground. The other two men were trying to catch hold of him, but he was surprisingly quick and wriggly. Grandpa Frank and I darted over to him and tried to help him to his feet, but then Mr Kay's guys grabbed hold of us.

Grandpa Frank shouted, "Get off my grandson!"

And I shouted, "Get off my grandpa!"

Meanwhile, Tony, who was still pinned under Mum, started yelling and shouting for help. He was doing his best to wrestle her off, but she'd started throwing a few punches about and was definitely getting the better of him.

Mr Kay wasn't impressed. He said, "Can everybody stop pratting about? This is not how I work!" Then he grabbed Mum quite roughly and pulled her off Tony.

From wherever Dicky was watching, he mustn't have been happy at seeing Mum being mishandled. Both Grandpa Frank and I heard his howl and we both knew what was coming. Dicky bounded out from between a row of parked cars, heading across the car park – followed by Janice, Paul and Dave – straight for Mr Kay.

When Mr Kay spotted him, he let go of Mum, held his hands up and said, "What in the holy hounds of hell is that?"

Grandpa Frank smiled and said, "That's Dicky. He's my dog and he doesn't seem pleased."

Mr Kay opened his mouth again, but before he could say anything else, Dicky took a giant leap and hurled himself at the man. Mr Kay hit the tarmac with quite a wallop. Dicky put his massive paws on Mr Kay's chest, pressed his nose onto Mr Kay's nose and growled.

So there we all were – Dad **caterpillaring** on his belly, Grandpa Frank and me trying to **wrestle** free from the clutches of Mr Kay's men, Mum **swinging** punches at Tony, Mr Kay being **pinned** to the ground by Dicky and Janice, Paul and Dave just sort of **onlooking** – which, thinking about it, wasn't the most useful thing they could have been doing.

And this is exactly what was going on when we were all startled by the ear-piercing blast of a whistle.

CHAPTER 39

Never underestimate old people

Everyone stopped their **wrestling** and **punching** and **caterpillaring** and **unhelpful onlooking**. Even Dicky stopped growling to see who the whistle-blaster was.

The whistle-blaster was standing by the blacked-out SUV we had flown over earlier. She was wearing a black velour tracksuit and a lot of make-up, and had hair like lilac candyfloss and wrinkly skin like a sultana. She didn't look pleased. She didn't sound pleased either. She said, "I am not pleased by what I am witnessing. Not pleased at all."

Grandpa Frank rearranged his deerstalker and said,

"I do not believe what my eyes are telling me – *Florence?*"

"Synchronized-swimming Florence! What are you doing here?" I said.

"Aunty Flo," Mr Kay said.

"Aunty Flo?" everyone else said, because it was all very confusing.

She blew her whistle again and said, "Big dog, down!" Understandably, Dicky did as he was told. Then she stalked over to Mr Kay, pointing her wrinkly finger at him. "This was supposed to be a standard job – get the money and go, I told you. But somehow you've managed, as usual, to turn it into a boondoggle of epic proportions."

Mr Kay looked at the floor and said, "I'm sorry, Aunty Flo."

Grandpa Frank said, "Florence, you know these men?"

"They're my nephews. They work for my loan company."

I couldn't help blurting out, "I thought you were a synchronized-swimming coach, not the head of an illegal money-lending operation."

Florence studied her red-painted fingernails, then looked at me and said, "A woman can be both."

It seemed like an unusual combination, but if I'd learned anything, it was that **you should never underestimate old people**.

Florence hadn't finished with Mr Kay. "Tell me, Robert," she said, "what exactly were you intending to do here?"

Mr Kay pointed at Dad, who, by this point, had made it quite some distance across the car park on his belly. "We were going to hold him over the edge until he gave us the money."

Florence took a deep breath. "And what were you going to do when he didn't hand it over? Drop him?"

Mr Kay shrugged. "I s'pose."

"In broad daylight?"

Mr Kay looked over at Tony and the two other guys, but they wouldn't meet his eyes.

"And how," continued Florence, "do you propose you'd get my money from him then?"

Mr Kay shifted from foot to foot. "It would be difficult."

"And how, when a crowd of Grigsby's shoppers had gathered to inspect the flattened body, would you expect to get away without any witnesses?" Florence flicked Mr Kay on the forehead after she'd said that. I couldn't help it, but that made me laugh. Mr Kay was getting a right dressing-down.

"That might have been a bit of a problem too," Mr Kay admitted.

"This is not the sort of money-lending operation that I run, Robert. We're a family business."

Florence looked from me to Grandpa Frank to Mum to Dad and then the others, and said, "Now what do we do about *this* situation?"

Tony said, "We can get rid of all of them if you want, Mrs Kay. So there are no witnesses."

That didn't sound wonderful for us.

Grandpa Frank said, "That doesn't seem very family-business-like."

And luckily, Florence said, "I agree, and it just so happens that I have a better idea." She walked over to Grandpa Frank, wiggled his ear flaps and said, "Let's talk synchro."

Money isn't everything

Dad had always led me to believe that money is the most important thing in the world. I suppose, when I was after the reward, I had started to think like that too. Luckily for Dad, Florence Kay – head coach of **The Dolphins Masters Synchronized Swimming Team** and boss of the **Kay Family Loan Company** – didn't think money was the most important thing in the world.

No, for Florence, it was synchronized swimming.

And, for some reason, she thought Grandpa Frank was the answer to all her aquatic-based prayers.

"I want you, Frank," she said. "Never have I seen

someone with such innate ability in the water. You. Are. Special."

Dad, who was still belly-down on the floor at this point, said, **"You what?"**

And Tony and Mr Kay and the other Kays said, **"You what?"**

And Balloon Dave and Janice and Paul said, **"You what?"**

And Dicky tilted his huge head to the side and made a doggy noise which sounded very much like, **"You what?"**

And Mum said, "I'm sorry, you've lost me, for a moment I thought you were saying you want Frank for a synchronized-swimming team."

And Florence Kay looked at Grandpa Frank and said, "I do."

And Grandpa Frank said, "Alright then, but it will cost you."

And Florence said, "How about two hundred grand?"

And in that moment Grandpa Frank became the highest paid veteran athlete in history.

CHAPTER 41

Sometimes, you just have to give it a go

After Grandpa Frank and Florence Kay had sealed the deal with a handshake, Tony opened the doors to the car park, which Mr Kay and the others had barricaded shut for the hostaging. A whole load of bewildered Grigsby's customers spilled onto the roof to get their cars and were very surprised to see a hot-air balloon taking off, as Balloon Dave made his exit (I think he was keen to get away from Mum before she demanded another lift).

Mum went into work mode – her customer-service training kicking into action. She said, "I'm Tanya Davenport, Grigsby's supervisor. Please move along, there's nothing to see here," which I don't think anyone was buying, but she did manage to stop the situation becoming any more of a commotion. She can be quite forceful when she puts her mind to it.

We all waved goodbye to Dad's kidnappers and they disappeared off in their black Hummer.

Janice and Paul went off with Dicky to retrieve the dogmobile, which was still parked somewhere on the A205, which left me, Grandpa Frank, Mum and Dad. Nobody said anything for a while. I guess it was hard to know what to say first.

Eventually, Dad said, "I guess I'll call for a taxi to take us home. It's been a bit of a day."

Mum folded her arms. "Oh, it's not over for you yet, sunshine. Not by a long shot. We've got some talking to do."

When the taxi came, Mum gave Grandpa Frank a big hug and a kiss and said, "Thank you for today. You were wonderful."

I thought Dad was going to thank him too – that they'd make friends again and everything would be better – but he didn't. He looked at Grandpa Frank like he was going to say something, but he opened his mouth, closed it again and then just nodded.

Grandpa Frank said, "It's okay, son. I know."

Dad swallowed and put his arm around me. "Come on, Frank. Get in the cab. Let's go home."

That was it? I couldn't believe it! "Are you *actually* kidding right now?" I spluttered, knocking his arm away. "Grandpa Frank just jumped out of a hot-air balloon for you. He's agreed to an intense synchronized-swimming training programme for you. He *saved* you. And all you can do is nod?"

"We're all tired, Frank. No one wants some big overemotional scene."

He might not have wanted one, but he was going to get one. "I'm not getting in that taxi because it's not taking me home. I told you, my home is at Autumnal Leaves." I think I might have even stamped my foot for effect.

I thought Dad was going to tell me I was being ridiculous again, but before he could speak, Mum leaned out of the car door and said, "Frank, he's got a point."

Both Dad and I said, "I do?" because Mum never usually thinks either of us have a point.

"Not you, him," she said, pointing at me. "Think about it, Frank. Living in that big place, you could have a job – a proper one and all. You could stop all your wheeling and dealing!"

"What are you saying, Tan?"

"I'm saying Frank can't look after all those old people on his own, can you, love?"

I said, "I can! I'm excellent at looking after old people." Then I realized what she was getting at and back-pedalled. "But some of them can be pretty difficult. Would be good to have a hand."

"How's about it, Frank? What if we all move in there together? We could have a proper good go at being a family."

Grandpa Frank said, "I mean, that would be wonderful. What do you say, son? You want to give me a chance to make up for lost time?"

Before Dad could answer, Mum said, "I don't even know why I'm asking you. We're doing it. Now would everybody get in the taxi, the meter's running."

Dad knew when he was beaten. He looked at me and shrugged.

I shrugged back at him.

Then he smiled this big real smile, ruffled my hair and said, "The sun is shining, birds are doing their tweetin'. It's a great day for a father to spend time with his favourite son."

And Grandpa Frank said, "Ain't that the truth."

Dad opened the taxi door. "Come on then, Dad, let's go home."

Grandpa Frank climbed in, took off his hat and dabbed his eyes with the ear flaps. "Well, today's a day I won't forget."

He did though.

CHAPTER 42

We all need looking after

We all moved in together and the Davenport family became the owners of Autumnal Leaves Retirement Home. I'd got it for an absolute bargain, to be honest. The owner, some guy called Eric, wanted the money fast. Much later, I'd heard a rumour that he'd done a runner after upsetting a money-lending gang headed by someone called "The Whistler". So maybe Florence helped us out more than once.

Luckily, Mum, Dad and Stephen were very on board with my vision for us to provide quality entertainment for old folk and we installed a climbing wall, a state-of-the-art gym, one of those ice-cream factory machines you get at Pizza Hut and a room just for laser tag. I don't think I'm exaggerating when I say Autumnal Leaves is definitely the best old people's home in the entire galaxy. And because all the wrinklies were happy, no one tried to break out and I didn't need to put up an electric perimeter fence.

Grandpa Frank turned out to be worth his sign-up fee of two hundred thousand pounds, because the Dolphins won gold at the old people's national championships two years running and Florence Kay was delighted. She injected a lot of cash into Autumnal Leaves because she thought it was an excellent source of more synchronized-swimming talent. We bus all the residents to the pool twice a week for training. **The Dolphins** now have over thirty members.

After a while, Grandpa Frank had to stop swimming. It got too much for him. A lot of things got too much for him. It was his mind, you see. Sometimes he'd know who we were, but most of the time he didn't. It made me very sad, but it didn't stop me from loving him. He was still my Grandpa Frank and my best friend, and I was still his grandson.

He and Dad never did have a conversation about why they fell out. They didn't talk things over. They just began again.

Dad says he wishes he'd made up with him sooner, but I guess we don't often say the right things at the right times. Sometimes, we say them too late. Sometimes, we don't say them at all. But sometimes, if we're lucky, we get to hear what we need to hear, even if it's in a way we're not expecting.

I went to see Grandpa Frank in the lounge not long before it happened. While the other residents were outside playing a game of dodgeball, Stephen had set him up with paints and a canvas and said to him, "**Why don't you paint what makes you happy?**"

I pulled up my footstool, gave Dicky a stroke and said, "How are you doing, Grandpa Frank?"

He dabbed a little more paint on his picture, then looked up and said, "Hello, son, where's your brother Vinny?"

"He's in Ireland working on the fair, Grandpa Frank."

"Is that so?"

He looked a bit upset, which happened when he got confused, so I changed the subject. "What's all this you're painting?"

He frowned at his work. "I don't really know. Can't make armpit nor elbow of it."

Granted, Grandpa Frank wasn't the most wonderful of artists, but I could work out what he had painted. There was a hot-air balloon and a monster truck and a pond full of Canada geese and a swimming pool full of pineapples (which I guess was the Dolphins synchro team), a picture of a stick man jumping off a very high wall (I think some artistic licence went into that) and Dicky and Patricia the poodle, and Mum in her silver coat, looking a bit like Patricia the poodle.

And there was me and Dad and Grandpa Frank, together watching Charlton at the Valley.

He had painted our **Bucket List**.

What he said next makes me wonder if he knew what was coming, because he said, "I think I lived my best life, didn't I, son?"

I said, "You certainly did, Grandpa Frank. The best."

Dad came in at this point with a pack of frozen peas

pressed to his forehead. He said, "That Brenda can really throw a ball." Then he looked at Grandpa Frank's painting and said, "Now, isn't that something!"

Grandpa Frank held out his hand and said, "Frank Davenport Senior, pleasure to meet you."

Dad smiled and said, "A real pleasure to meet you too, sir."

"This here is my son, also called Frank," Grandpa Frank went on. "The name Frank – it's a family tradition. He's the most brilliant boy. I'm so proud of him. Couldn't love him more if I tried. I don't think I tell him that enough. I hope he knows."

Dad took a breath before saying, in a slightly wobbly voice, "Well, I think he does now," and he leaned forward and gave Grandpa Frank a kiss on the cheek and a hug and said, "I love you, Dad."

He cleared his throat and walked out the room, blinking his eyes, because he still believed Davenport men don't cry.

After he had gone, Grandpa Frank frowned at me and said, "Well, wasn't he a funny fella?"

I've got that painting in my bedroom now. It hangs on the wall over Grandpa Frank's deerstalker hat. Every time I look at it, I realize something new.

Like that sometimes you have to change your point of view to understand things. Go way up high in a hot-air balloon, for instance.

Or that caring for others – including massive dogs – can actually bring *you* happiness.

And that you should always have a go at things, even if you're embarrassed, because, you never know, you might be excellent (once you're in it, a sequined swimsuit really isn't *too* terrible).

That sometimes you have to attack things head-on, especially any walls that are blocking your way.

And that it's not always the big things that can get you – you have to watch out for the little things too, even if you're driving a monster truck and feel invincible.

And that people are going to make mistakes, so it's probably best to forgive them.

But mostly it reminds me, every day, to live my best life.

It wasn't long after he'd died that Mr Foster turned up at Autumnal Leaves' reception to talk about Grandpa Frank's will. As he was leaving, he said, "I'm sorry that I only remembered to look into this after your grandpa had passed, but there is one more thing I need to talk to you about. I couldn't find anything in your grandmother Nora's assets that could be a reward for looking after him. There just doesn't seem to be one."

And I thought about everything we'd done and everything I'd gained and said, "That's where you're wrong."

My name is Frank Davenport, just like my dad. And just like my grandpa. And that was the story of **our Great Big Bucket List**.

THE END

KNOW YOUR OLDIES!

Guess the age of these exceptional old people...

At eighty years old, Grandpa Frank proves that hot-air balloon rides, monster-truck lessons and epic parkour experiences aren't just for kids. Can you guess the ages of these other exceptional older people?

1. Dickie Borthwick is the UK's oldest footballer, having played in over 1,600 games since 1948. How old is Dickie?

2. Having danced her whole life, Barbara Peters returned to ballet lessons in 2015 and is officially Britain's oldest ballerina. Can you guess how old Barbara is?

3. He is better known for walking 100 laps of his garden raising £39 million for NHS Charities Together,

but how old was legendary Captain Tom Moore when he became the oldest person to reach No.1 on the UK's Official Singles Chart?

4. Doris Cicely Long took up abseiling aged 85, but how old was she when she abseiled the 170 m (560 ft) Spinnaker Tower in Portsmouth, UK, on 12 July 2015?

5. Hamako Mori, the "Gamer Grandma', played her first video game in 1981 and is now officially recognized as the oldest gaming YouTuber in the world. How old is the Gamer Grandma?

6. By day Sumiko Iwamura serves food in her restaurant, but by night she becomes DJ Sumirock, playing to crowds on the dancefloor. What age do you think Sumiko, the oldest professional club DJ, is?

Answers (as of 2021)

1. 85 years old

2. 83 years old

3. 99 years old

4. 101 years old

5. 91 years old

6. 86 years old

THINGS TO DO IN YOUR COMMUNITY

When Frank meets the old people at **Autumnal Leaves**, he wants to do whatever he can to help them. But you don't need a games room or a hot-air balloon to do the same. Here are some ideas for things you can do in your community to help older people.

- Join **The innocent Big Knit** by knitting little hats for smoothie bottles, which help raise money for older people. Take your knitted hats to your local **Age UK** charity shop and they'll do the rest!

- Ask your parents if you can host a tea party for local older people with **Re:Engage**, a charity that supports older people through volunteering.

- Ask your teacher if your class can take part in **My Dear New Friend**, a National Literacy Trust project. This project encourages children to write letters to older people living in care homes.

A NOTE FROM JENNY

Dear Reader,

I have been very lucky to have four wonderful grandparents, who have all been a huge part of my life, full of wisdom, brilliance and, most importantly, fun. But it can be a worrying time to see a grandparent getting older, and sometimes, becoming unwell and sadly coming to the end of their life – as Grandpa Frank does at the end of this story.

If you ever have any worries or questions about your grandparents as they grow older, please do talk to your parents, guardians, teachers or an adult you trust, as they will be able to listen to what is worrying you. They can also help you find support online, including charities who can answer questions or discuss worries about illnesses, such as dementia, and with bereavement.

As a grandparent gets older or becomes unwell, it can mean that they might not be able to go monster-trucking or parkouring with you, but that doesn't mean you can't find ways to spend time together. And it doesn't mean that they love you any less.

When someone you love dies, there are also lots of ways you can keep memories alive. You can sing their favourite songs, enjoy sharing their favourite foods, tell jokes they used to tell and share memories with your family and friends. Frank keeps a few of the things that were special to Grandpa Frank, and he can have a look at them any time he is thinking about his grandpa. Their bond remains even though they aren't together any more, and that's the special thing about love, you carry it inside of you always.

Jenny Pearson

Watch out for more **HILARIOUS** and
HEART-WARMING books by
JENNY PEARSON...

"This sleuthing-trip-cum-crime-
solving spree has all the fizz of
Jeremy Strong." **The Observer**

"As funny and tender as it could ever be."
Frank Cottrell-Boyce

"A comic romp packed with record-breaking
stunts and satire."
**The Times, Children's Book
of the Week**

Acknowledgements

I have been very lucky to have been blessed with fabulous grandparents and I owe much of the humour and heart in this book to them. I must thank those departed, my grandad David Browne and my nanny Iris Browne, and those still very much living, my grandad John Grigsby and nanny Brenda Grigsby, who have been a constant source of support throughout my life. Thank you. I love you.

My own children also have excellent grandparents in my dad David Browne and my step-mother Eleanor Browne, my mum Jeanette Smith and my late step-father Hugh Smith, and Mike and Helen Pearson.

As I'm thanking family, I'll get into enormous trouble if I don't mention Andrew, William and Douglas and my sister, Caroline, for their unwavering support.

To my incredible editors, Rebecca Hill and Becky Walker. It is a constant joy that I get to work with the best in the business.

David O'Connell, your illustrations are absolutely perfect. I cannot thank you enough for the humour and joy that you have brought to the page. I will always laugh at the pineapple swimmers.

Thanks also to Peter and Nicola Usborne. I am honoured to be one of your authors and part of the Usborne family.

Jenny Tyler, thank you for your support and belief in my books. It isn't unnoticed and it is hugely appreciated.

Joanna Olney, Katarina Jovanovic, Fritha Lindqvist; each and every time you blow me away with how you manage to get me and my books out there. Thank you.

Katharine Millichope, queen of design, thank you so much for making Grandpa Frank look fabulous.

To Christian Herisson and Arfana Islam, Sarah Cronin and Lauren Robertson, Sarah Stewart and Jessica Feichtlbauer and everybody at Usborne, thank you so much for all that you do.

I must also thank my friend Samantha Holder and her mum Jill Ladd, who provided much inspiration for this story with the "90 things to do when you're 90" adventure they had with Sam's grandfather, Arthur Absalom. A true gentleman and incredibly good sport.

Thank you to my school friends, Cassie, Deci, Debbie, Gayle, Lily, Louise and Josie, and to my friend Laura Joyes for always shouting loudly about my books and keeping me sane.

Thanks also to David Joyes for the link up with Charlton and to Ravi Patel and the team at Charlton Athletic Football Club (Go on you Addicks!) for your support in launching this book.

Thanks also to Charlie Barrow, Charlton Athletic fan and advisor on all things Charlton related.

Ellie and David Parsons, thank you too for pushing my books and being truly excellent people.

To all the wonderful teachers and educationalists, who share my books: Andrew Rough, Ben Harris, Ceridwen Eccles, Chris Soul, Chris Youles, Dean Boddington (total babe), Emily Weston, Emma Kuyateh, Erin Hamilton, Jacqui Sydney, James Haddell, Jen O'Brien, John Hughes, Jon Biddle, Kate Heap, Kevin Cobane, Mark Clutterbuck, Martin Jones, Miss Bishop, Miss Cleveland, Miss Gibson, Nicola Squares, Richard Simpson, Rumena Aktar, Sam Fuller, Scott Evans, Tom Griffiths, Tom Slattery, Valda Varadinek, Amanda Harvey, Mr Tarrant and so many more!

And to teachers and pupils at my own school, St Margaret's in Durham.

To Fiona Sharp, in Waterstones Durham; your support is so appreciated. You don't let the fact that someone already has a copy stop you from selling them another. You even managed to sell a Welsh translation! This needs formal acknowledgement. Thank you also to Kat and the rest of the Durham team.

Also to lovely Jo Bower at the Rocketship, Helen Tamblyn-Saville at Wonderland, Helen Stanton at Forum books and The Bound. And to Henrietta Englefield, librarian extraordinaire at Colfe's, for her support and walking 100km for Our Time having been inspired to do so by *The Incredible Record Smashers*.

Final thanks to the wonder that is my agent, Sam Copeland, who believed in this book (and me) right from the very start.